'Robert Seethaler's quietly mesmerizing novel – elemental in both tone and subject – shows what joy and nobility can be found in a life of hardship, patience and bereavement. It is at once heart-rending and heart-warming. *A Whole Life*, for all its gentleness, is a very powerful book'

JIM CRACE

'Against the backdrop of a literary world that often seems crowded with novels yelling "Look at me!", it's refreshing to read a story marked by quiet, concentrated attention . . . What is perhaps most remarkable about this remarkable novel is the way that it continually weaves past, present and future into a single fabric . . . Deeply moving'

Sunday Times

'The solitude and remoteness of the mountains inspire remarkable, contemplative passages . . . The book's prose has a directness and detail that helps to set off the moments of genuine wisdom and restrained poetry, all of which makes Charlotte Collins's translation a great triumph. It is at this point that you realize why the novella should be doing so well in Germany, and why it is so urgent for the rest of us: it can guide its readers to make the best of their lives, however they turn out'

Sunday Telegraph

Robert Seethaler

A Whole Life

Translated by Charlotte Collins

PICADOR

First published 2015 by Picador

First published in paperback 2015 by Picador
an imprint of Pan Macmillan
20 New Wharf Road, London N1 9RR
Associated companies throughout the world
www.panmacmillan.com

ISBN 978-1-4472-8390-4

3 5 7 9 8 6 4

A CIP catalogue record for this book is available from the British Library.

Printed and bound by CPI Group (UK) Ltd, Croydon, CR0 4YY

Visit **www.picador.com** to read more about all our books
and to buy them. You will also find features, author interviews and
news of any author events, and you can sign up for e-newsletters
so that you're always first to hear about our new releases.

A Whole Life

On a February morning in the year 1933 Andreas Egger lifted the dying goatherd Johannes Kalischka, known to all the valley dwellers as Horned Hannes, off his sodden and rather sour-smelling pallet to carry him down to the village along the three-kilometre mountain path that lay buried beneath a thick layer of snow.

A strange intuition had prompted him to call on Horned Hannes in his hut, where he found him behind the stove, which had long since gone out, curled up under a heap of old goatskins. The goatherd stared at him out of the darkness, emaciated and ghostly pale, and Egger knew that Death already crouched behind his eyes. He picked him up in both arms like a child and placed him gently on the wooden frame, padded with dry moss, that Horned Hannes had used all his life to carry firewood and injured goats on his back over the hillside. He wrapped a halter around his body, tied it to the frame and pulled the knots so tight that the wood let out a crack. When he asked him if he was in pain, Horned Hannes shook his head and twisted his mouth into a grin, but Egger knew that he was lying.

The first weeks of the year had been unusually warm. The snow in the valleys had melted and in the village there was a constant dripping and splashing of meltwater. But a few days earlier it had turned icy-cold again, and the snow fell so thickly and incessantly from the sky that it seemed softly to swallow the landscape, smothering all life and sound. For the first few hundred metres Egger didn't speak to the trembling man on his back. He had enough to do keeping an eye on the path, which wound down the mountain in front of him in steep hairpin bends and was barely discernible in the driving snow. From time to time he felt Horned Hannes stirring. 'Just don't die on me now,' he said aloud, to himself, not expecting an answer. However, after he had been walking for almost half an hour with only the sound of his own panting in his ears, the answer came from behind: 'Dying wouldn't be the worst.'

'But not on my back!' said Egger, stopping to adjust the leather straps on his shoulders. For a moment he listened out into the soundlessly falling snow. The silence was absolute. It was the silence of the mountains that he knew so well, but which still had the capacity to fill his heart with fear. 'Not on my back,' he repeated, and walked on. After each bend in the path the snow seemed to fall even more thickly, relentlessly, soft and entirely without noise. Behind him Horned Hannes stirred less and less frequently, until at last he didn't move at all and Egger feared the worst.

'Are you dead?' he asked.

'No, you limping devil!' came the reply, with surprising clarity.

'All I mean is, you have to hold on till we get to the village. Then you can do whatever you want.'

'And what if I don't want to hold on till we get to the village?'

'You must!' said Egger. He felt they'd talked enough now, and for the next half-hour they progressed in silence. Almost three hundred metres above the village, beside the Geierkante, where the first mountain pines stooped like hunchbacked dwarves beneath the snow, Egger strayed from the path, stumbled, landed on the seat of his trousers and slid some twenty metres down the slope before he was stopped by a boulder as tall as a man. It was calm in the lee of the rock, and here the snow seemed to fall even more slowly, even more quietly. Egger sat on his bottom, leaning back slightly against the wooden frame. There was a stabbing pain in his left knee, but it was bearable and his leg was still in one piece. For a while Horned Hannes didn't move; then suddenly he began to cough and eventually to speak in a hoarse voice so quiet he could barely be understood: 'Where do you want to lie, Andreas Egger?'

'What?'

'What earth do you want to be buried in?'

'I don't know,' said Egger. He had never considered this question, and in fact in his opinion there was no point wasting any time or thought on such things. 'The earth is the earth; it makes no difference where you lie.'

'Maybe it makes no difference the way nothing makes any difference in the end,' he heard Horned Hannes whisper. 'But there will be a cold. A cold that gnaws the bones. And the soul.'

'The soul too?' asked Egger, and a sudden shiver ran down his spine.

'The soul most of all!' answered Horned Hannes. He had stretched his head out as far as he could around the edge of the frame and was staring at the wall of fog and falling snow. 'The soul and the bones and the spirit and everything you've been attached to and believed in all your life. The eternal cold will gnaw it all away. That's what's written, because that's what I've heard. People say death brings forth new life, but people are stupider than the stupidest nanny goat. I say death brings forth nothing at all! Death is the Cold Lady.'

'The . . . what?'

'The Cold Lady,' repeated Horned Hannes. 'She walks on the mountain and steals through the valley. She comes when she wants and takes what she needs. She has no face and no voice. The Cold Lady comes and takes and goes. That's all. She seizes you as she passes and takes you with her and sticks you in some hole. And in the last patch of sky you see before they finally shovel the earth in over you she reappears and breathes on you. And all that's left for you then is darkness. And the cold.'

Egger looked up into the snowy sky and for a moment he feared something might appear there and breathe in his face. 'Jesus,' he muttered, through clenched teeth. 'That's bad.'

'Yes, it's bad,' said Horned Hannes, and his voice sounded raw with fear. Neither man stirred again. The silence was now overlaid by the quiet singing of the wind as it swept over the ridge, dusting up wispy pennants of snow. Suddenly Egger felt a movement, and a moment later he tipped over backwards and lay on his back in the snow. Horned Hannes had somehow managed to loosen the knots and, quick as a flash, clamber out of the frame. He stood there, spindly beneath his ragged clothes and swaying slightly in the wind. Egger shuddered again. 'You get straight back in,' he said. 'You'll catch something else otherwise.'

Horned Hannes paused, his head craned forward. For a moment he seemed still to be listening to Egger's words, but the snow had swallowed them. Then he turned and began to run up the mountain in great leaps. Egger struggled to his feet, slipped, fell again, cursing, onto his back, pushed himself up off the ground with both hands and got to his feet once more. 'Come back!' he yelled after the goatherd, who was bounding away with astonishing speed. But Horned Hannes could no longer hear him. Egger slipped the straps off his shoulders, dropped the frame and ran after him, but after only a few metres he had to stop, gasping for breath: the slope was too steep here, and with every step he sank up to his hips in the snow. The scrawny figure ahead of him quickly diminished until at last it dissolved entirely in the impenetrable whiteness of the blizzard. Egger put his hands to his mouth like a funnel and shouted at the top of his voice, 'Stop, you stupid fool! No one has ever outrun Death!' To no avail: Horned Hannes had disappeared.

Andreas Egger walked the last few hundred metres down to the village to revive his profoundly shaken spirits with a bowl of greasy doughnuts and a glass of homemade Krauterer at the Golden Goat inn. He found himself a spot right beside the old tiled stove, placed his hands on the table and felt the warm blood flow slowly back to his fingers. The little door of the stove stood open and the fire crackled inside. For a brief moment he thought he saw the face of the goatherd in the flames, staring out at him, unmoving. Quickly he closed the door and knocked back his schnapps with his eyes screwed tightly shut. When he opened them again a young woman was standing in front of him. She just stood there, hands on her hips, looking at him. Her hair was short and flaxen blonde, and her skin shone rosy in the warmth of the stove. Egger was reminded of the newborn piglets he had sometimes picked out of the straw when he was a boy, burying his face in their soft bellies that smelled of earth, milk and pig muck. He glanced down at his hands. Suddenly they seemed strange to him, lying there: heavy, useless and stupid.

'Another one?' the young woman asked, and Egger nodded. She brought a fresh glass, and as she leaned forward to put it on the table she touched his upper arm with a fold of her blouse. The touch was barely perceptible, yet it left a subtle pain that seemed to sink deeper into his flesh with every passing second. He looked at her, and she smiled.

All his life Andreas Egger would look back on this moment, again and again: that brief smile that afternoon in front of the quietly crackling guesthouse stove.

Later, when he stepped back out into the open, it had already stopped snowing. It was cold and the air was clear. Scraps of fog were creeping up the mountains, and the peaks were already glowing in the sun. Egger left the village behind him and trudged home through the deep snow. A group of children were playing by the mountain stream a few metres beyond the old wooden footbridge. They had tossed their schoolbags into the snow and were scrambling about in the bed of the brook. Some were sliding down the frozen watercourse on their bottoms while others crept across the ice on all fours, listening to the quiet burbling beneath. When they spotted Egger they ganged up and started shouting, 'Gammy Leg! Gammy Leg!' Their voices rang out bright and clear in the glassy air, like the cries of the young golden eagles that circled high above the valley, plucking fallen chamois from ravines and goats from the pasture. 'Gammy Leg! Gammy Leg!' Egger put down the wooden frame, broke off a fist-sized chunk of ice from the overhanging bank of the stream, drew his arm back and flung it in their direction. He aimed far too high, and the chunk of ice sailed well over the children's heads. For a moment, at the highest point of its trajectory, it looked as if it would just hang there, a small celestial body flashing in the sun. Then it plunged down and disappeared soundlessly in the shadow of the snowbound fir trees.

* * *

Three months later Egger was sitting on a tree stump at the exact same spot, watching a yellowish cloud of dust darken the mouth of the valley, from which, moments later, the construction team of the firm Bittermann and

Sons – consisting of two hundred and sixty labourers, twelve machinists, four engineers, seven Italian cooks and a small number of unspecified auxiliary staff – emerged and approached the village. From a distance the throng resembled an enormous herd of cattle; only by squinting was it possible to discern, here and there, a raised arm or a pickaxe carried over a shoulder. This group was merely the vanguard of a convoy of heavy horse-drawn vehicles and trucks loaded with machines, tools, steel girders, cement and other building materials that proceeded along the unpaved road at walking speed. For the first time the muffled rattle of diesel engines reverberated through the valley. The locals stood silently by the side of the road, until suddenly the old stable hand Joseph Malitzer snatched his felt hat from his head and flung it into the air with a shout of delight. Now the others also began shouting, cheering, yelling. For weeks they had been waiting for the onset of spring, and with it the arrival of the construction team. A cable car was to be built. An aerial cable car powered by direct-current electricity, in whose light-blue wooden cabins people would float up the mountain, enjoying a panoramic view of the whole valley. It was a massive undertaking. Cables twenty-five millimetres thick and intertwined like pairs of mating adders would slice through the sky across a distance of almost two thousand metres. There was a difference in altitude of one thousand three hundred metres to overcome; there were gorges to be bridged and overhanging rocks to be blasted. With the cable car, electricity too would come to the valley. Electric current would flow in along buzzing cables and all the streets and houses and barns would glow with warm light, even at night. People were thinking of all this and much more as they threw up their hats and sent their shouts of delight up into the clear air. Egger would have liked to cheer with them, but for some reason he stayed sitting on his tree stump. He felt despondent, without knowing why. Perhaps it had something to do with the rattling of the engines, the noise that suddenly filled the valley. Nobody knew when it would go away again, or whether it ever would go away again. For a while Egger remained seated: then he couldn't hold out any longer. He jumped up, ran down, joined the others by the side of the road and shouted and cheered as loudly as he could.

As a child Andreas Egger had never shouted or cheered. He didn't even really talk until his first year at school.

With difficulty he had scraped together a handful of words that at rare moments he would recite in random order. Talking meant attracting attention, which was never a good thing. He arrived in the village as a small boy in the summer of 1902, brought by horse-drawn carriage from a town far beyond the mountains. When he was lifted out he stood there, speechless, eyes wide, gazing up in astonishment at the shimmering white peaks. He must have been about four years old at the time, perhaps a little younger or older. No one knew exactly, and no one was interested, least of all the farmer Hubert Kranzstocker, who reluctantly took receipt of little Egger and gave the carriage driver the measly tip of two groschen and a crust of hard bread. The lad was the only child of one of his sisters-in-law; she had led an irresponsible life, for which God had recently punished her with consumption and summoned her to his bosom. At least there was a leather pouch around the boy's neck with a few bank notes in it. For Kranzstocker, this was reason enough not to tell him to go to the devil, or leave him at the church door for the priest, which came to much the same thing in his opinion. So now here Egger stood, gazing at the mountains in wonder. This was the only image he retained of his early childhood, and he carried it with him throughout his life. There were no memories of the time before, and at some point the years that followed, his early years on the Kranzstocker farm, also dissolved in the mists of the past.

In his next memory he saw himself as a boy of about eight, skinny and naked, hanging over the yoke of the plough. His legs and his head dangled just above the ground, which stank of horse piss, while his small white bottom jutted up into the winter air and received Kranzstocker's blows with the hazel rod. As he always did, the farmer had bathed the rod in water to render it supple. Now it hissed briefly and sharply through the air before landing with a sigh on Egger's backside. Egger never screamed, which only spurred the farmer on to thrash him harder. Man was formed and hardened by God's hand to subdue the Earth and all that moves upon it. Man carries out God's will and speaks God's word. Man creates life with the strength of his loins, and takes life with the strength of his arms. Man is flesh and he is earth and he is a farmer and his name is Hubert Kranzstocker. When it pleases him so to do he digs his field, grabs a full-grown sow and hoists it onto his shoulders, begets a child or hangs another over the yoke of the plough, for he is the man, the word and the deed. 'Lordhavemercy,' said Kranzstocker, and brought the rod whistling down. 'Lordhavemercy.'

There were reasons enough for these beatings: spilt milk, mouldy bread, a lost cow or an evening prayer wrongly stammered. Once the farmer cut the rod too thick, or had forgotten to soak it, or struck with greater fury than usual, it was hard to say exactly which: at any rate, he struck, and somewhere in the little body there was a loud crack and the boy stopped moving. 'Lordhavemercy,' said Kranzstocker, lowering his arm in astonishment. Little Egger was brought into the house, laid on the straw and brought back to life by the farmer's wife with a bucket of water and a beaker of warm milk. Something was out of place in his right leg, but as it would be too expensive to have it examined in a hospital the bonesetter Alois Klammerer was sent for from the neighbouring village. Alois Klammerer was a friendly man with unusually small, pale pink hands, but their strength and dexterity were legendary, even among woodcutters and blacksmiths. Once, years ago, he had been summoned to the Hirz family farm where the farmer's son, a monstrous young man with the strength of an ox, had crashed through the stable roof, drunk as a lord. He had been rolling around for hours in pain and chicken shit, emitting inarticulate noises and successfully deploying a pitchfork to defend himself against every intervention. Nimbly dodging the fork thrusts, Alois Klammerer approached him with a nonchalant smile, stabbed two fingers unerringly into the lad's nostrils and with one simple movement forced him to his knees, setting first his stubborn head and, immediately afterwards, his dislocated bones to rights.

The bonesetter Alois Klammerer also eased little Egger's broken thigh back together. Afterwards he splinted the leg with a couple of thin wooden laths, lubricated it with herbal ointment and wrapped it in a thick bandage. Egger had to spend the next six weeks on a straw mattress in the attic, relieving himself lying down, in an old cream bowl. Many years later, long after he had grown to manhood and was strong enough to carry a dying goatherd down the mountain on his back, Andreas Egger thought back to those nights in the attic and the stench of herbs, rat droppings and his own excreta. He felt the warmth of the room below rising up through the floorboards. He heard the farmer's children moaning softly in their sleep, Kranzstocker's rumbling snores, and the inscrutable sounds of his wife. The noises of the animals drifted up to him from the barn, their rustling, breathing, munching and snuffling. Sometimes, on bright nights when he couldn't fall asleep and the moon appeared in the little skylight, he tried to sit up as straight as possible to be closer to it. The moonlight was friendly and soft, and when he contemplated his toes in it they looked like small round lumps of cheese.

When the bonesetter was finally called back six weeks later to undo the bandage, the leg was as thin as a chicken bone. It also jutted out crookedly from the hip and seemed generally to have turned out a bit twisted and awry. 'It'll sort itself out, like everything in life,' said Klammerer, bathing his hands in a bowl of milk fresh from the cow. Little Egger bit back the pain, climbed out of bed, dragged himself out of the house and a little further, to the big chicken field where the primroses and leopard's bane were already in bloom. He slipped off his nightshirt and let himself fall backwards onto the grass with outstretched arms. The sun shone on his face, and for the first time he could remember he thought about his mother, whom he had not been able to picture for years. What must she have been like? What must it have been like for her, lying there, towards the end? All small and thin and white? With a single, trembling patch of sun on her brow?

Egger regained his strength. His leg, though, remained crooked, and from then on he went through life with a limp. It was as if his right leg always needed a moment longer than the rest of his body; as if before taking every step it first had to consider whether it really was worth the exertion.

Andreas Egger's memories of the childhood years that followed were frayed and fragmentary. Once he saw a mountain start to move. A jolt seemed to pass through the side in shadow, and with a deep groan the whole slope began to slide. The mass of earth swept away the forest chapel and a couple of haystacks, and buried beneath it the dilapidated walls of the abandoned Kernsteiner farm, which had been empty for years. A calf, separated from the herd because of an ulcer on its hind leg, was thrown high up into the air along with the cherry tree to which it was tethered: it gawped out over the valley for a moment before the scree surged in and swallowed it whole. Egger remembered people standing in front of their houses open-mouthed, watching the disaster unfold on the other side of the valley. The children held hands, the men were silent, the women wept, and everything was overlaid with the murmur of the old villagers reciting the Lord's Prayer. A few days later the calf was found a few hundred metres down the mountain, still tethered to the cherry tree, lying in a bend in the stream with a swollen belly, its stiff legs pointing at the sky and the water washing round it.

Egger shared the big bed in the bedroom with the farmer's children, but this didn't mean he was one of them. For the whole of his time on the farm he remained an outsider, barely tolerated, the bastard of a sister-in-law who had been punished by God, with only the contents of a leather neck pouch to thank for the farmer's clemency. To all intents and purposes he was not seen as a child. He was a creature whose function was to work, pray, and bare its bottom for the hazel rod. Only Nana, the farmer's wife's aged mother, spared him a warm look or a friendly word now and then. Sometimes she would place her hand on his head and murmur a quiet 'God bless you'. When Egger heard of her sudden death, during the haymaking – she had lost consciousness while baking bread, toppled forwards and suffocated with her face in the dough – he dropped his scythe, climbed wordlessly all the way up past the Adlerkante and looked for a shady spot to cry in.

Nana was laid out for three days in the little chamber between the farmhouse and the cattle shed. It was pitch dark in the room: the windows had been blacked out and the walls were hung with black cloths. Nana's hands were folded over a wooden rosary, her face lit by two flickering candles. The smell of decay quickly spread throughout the house; outside the summer was sweltering and the heat penetrated through every chink. When the hearse arrived, drawn by two enormous Haflingers, the farmer's family gathered around the body one last time to say goodbye. Kranzstocker sprinkled it with holy water, cleared his throat and muttered a few words. 'Nana's gone now,' he said. 'We can't know where to, but it'll be as it's meant to be. The old die, making way for new. That's how it is and how it'll always be, amen!' The body was hoisted onto the cart and the funeral procession, in which, as was the custom, the whole village participated, slowly began to move. They were just passing the smithy when its soot-covered door suddenly burst open and the smith's dog shot out into the open. Its fur was jet-black and between its legs its swollen, scarlet sex shone bright as a beacon. Barking hoarsely it hurtled towards the horses drawing the cart. The coachman flicked his whip across the dog's back, but it seemed to feel no pain. It leapt at one of the horses and sank its teeth into its hind leg. The Haflinger reared up and kicked out. Its enormous hoof hit the dog's head; there was a cracking noise, the dog yelped and fell like a sack to the ground. In front of the cart the injured horse staggered to one side, threatening to drag the carriage into the meltwater ditch. The coachman, who had leapt off the box and seized his animals' reins, managed to keep both cart and horses on the road, but at the back the coffin had slid and got stuck sideways. The lid had only been provisionally closed for transportation and was supposed to be nailed down at the graveside: it had sprung open, and the dead woman's forearm appeared in the gap. In the darkness of the viewing room her hand had been snow-white, but here, in the bright midday light, it appeared as yellow as the flowers of the little Alpine violets that blossomed on the shady banks of the stream and withered the instant they were exposed to the sun. The horse reared up one last time before coming to a standstill, flanks quivering. Egger saw Nana's dead hand dangling from the coffin, and for a moment it seemed she was trying to wave goodbye to him: a very last 'God bless you', meant for him alone. The lid was closed, the coffin pushed back into place, and the funeral procession was able to continue on its way. The dog stayed behind on the road where it lay on its side, shuddering convulsively, paddling in circles and snapping blindly at the air. The clacking of its jaw could be heard for quite some time, before the smith dashed its brains out with a peening anvil.

In 1910 a school was built in the village, and every morning, after tending to the livestock, little Egger sat with the other children, in a classroom that stank of fresh tar, learning reading, writing and arithmetic. He learned slowly and as if against a hidden, inner resistance, but over time a kind of meaning began to crystallize out of the chaos of dots and dashes on the school blackboard until at last he was able to read books without pictures, which awoke in him ideas and also certain anxieties about the worlds beyond the valley.

After the deaths of the two youngest Kranzstocker children, who were carried off one long winter's night by diphtheria, the work on the farm became even harder as there were fewer arms to share the burden. On the other hand, Egger had more space in the bed now, and no longer had to scrap over every crust with his remaining stepbrothers and stepsisters. He and the other children hardly came to blows any more, in any case, simply because Egger had grown too strong. It was as if Nature had been trying to make it up to him ever since the business with his shattered leg. At the age of thirteen he had the muscles of a young man, and at fourteen he heaved a sixty-kilo sack through the hatch to the granary for the first time. He was strong, but slow. He thought slowly, spoke slowly and walked slowly; yet every thought, every word and every step left a mark precisely where, in his opinion, such marks were supposed to be.

One day after Egger's eighteenth birthday (since no precise information could be obtained about his birth, the mayor had simply assigned a random summer date, namely the fifteenth of August 1898, as his birthday, and issued the certificate accordingly), an earthenware bowl of milk soup happened to slip out of his hands during supper, and broke with a dull crack. The soup, with the bread he had just crumbled into it, spread over the wooden floor, and Kranzstocker, who had already folded his hands to say grace, slowly rose to his feet. 'Fetch the hazel and put it in water,' he said. 'I'll see you in half an hour.'

Egger fetched the rod from its hook, put it outside in

the cattle trough, sat down on the yoke of the plough and dangled his legs. Half an hour later the farmer appeared. 'Bring the rod!' he said.

Egger jumped off the yoke and took the rod out of the trough. Kranzstocker brought it hissing down through the air. It flexed smoothly in his hand, trailing a curtain of delicately glittering water drops in its wake.

'Drop your trousers!' the farmer ordered. Egger folded his arms in front of his chest and shook his head.

'Well, look at you! The bastard wants to contradict the farmer,' said Kranzstocker.

'I want to be left alone, that's all,' said Egger.

The farmer thrust out his chin. There was dried milk stuck in the stubble of his beard. A long, curved vein throbbed in his neck. He stepped forward and raised his arm.

'If you hit me, I'll kill you!' said Egger, and the farmer froze.

In later life, when Egger looked back on this moment, it seemed to him that they stood like that the whole evening, confronting each other, he with his arms folded across his chest, the farmer with the hazel rod in his raised fist, both silent, with cold hatred in their eyes. In reality it was at most a few seconds. A drop of water ran slowly down the rod, trembled free and fell to earth. The cows' muffled chomping emanated from the barn. One of the children laughed inside the house, then the farm was quiet again.

Kranzstocker dropped his arm. 'Get out of here,' he said, in a toneless voice, and Egger went.

* * *

Andreas Egger was considered a cripple, but he was strong. He was a good worker, didn't ask for much, barely spoke, and tolerated the heat of the sun in the fields as well as the biting cold in the forest. He took on any kind of work and did it reliably and without grumbling. He was as good with a scythe as he was with a pitchfork. He turned the freshly mown grass, loaded dung onto carts, and lugged rocks and sheaves of straw from the fields. He crawled over the soil like a beetle and climbed between rocks to retrieve lost cattle. He knew in which direction to chop different kinds of wood, how to set the wedge, hone the saw and sharpen the axe. He seldom went to the inn, and he never allowed himself more than a meal and a glass of beer or a Krauterer. He scarcely spent a single night in a bed; usually he slept on hay, in attics, in small side rooms, and in barns, alongside the cattle. Sometimes, on mild summer nights, he would spread a blanket somewhere on a freshly mown meadow, lie on his back and look up at the starry sky. Then he would think about his future, which extended infinitely before him, precisely because he expected nothing of it. And sometimes, if he lay there long enough, he had the impression that beneath his back the earth was softly rising and falling, and in moments like these he knew that the mountains breathed.

By the time he was twenty-nine Egger had saved enough money to purchase the lease on a small plot of land with a hay barn. The patch of ground lay just below the tree line, about five hundred metres above the village, and could only be reached via the steep, narrow path to the Almerspitze. It was virtually worthless, steep and barren, littered with countless stones and scarcely bigger than the chicken field behind the Kranzstocker farm. But a little spring of clear, ice-cold water bubbled out of the rock nearby, and in the morning the sun stood on the ridge of the mountain half an hour earlier than in the village, warming the earth under Egger's night-damp feet. He felled a couple of trees in the surrounding forest, worked them on the spot and dragged the beams to his hay barn to prop up the crooked walls. For the foundation he dug a hole and filled it with the stones from his plot, which rather than decreasing in number seemed to grow back night after night out of the dry and dusty ground. He gathered the stones, and because he got bored doing it he gave them names. And when he ran out of names, he gave them words. And when at some point it became clear to him that there were more stones on his plot of land than he knew words, he just started again from the beginning. He needed no plough and no cattle. His plot was too small for a farm of his own, but it was big enough for a tiny vegetable garden. Right at the end he erected a low fence around his new home and put in a little gate, with the express intention of being able to hold it open one day for some potential visitor who might come calling.

All in all, it was a good time. Egger was content, and as far as he was concerned things could have gone on like that for ever. But then came the incident with Horned Hannes. According to his understanding of responsibility and justice, the goatherd's disappearance was not his fault; nonetheless, Egger told no one about what had happened in the thick of the blizzard. Horned Hannes was believed to be dead, and although his body was never found, not even Egger doubted it for a moment. Yet he could not forget the image of that spindly figure slowly dissolving into fog before his eyes.

There was something else that, since that day, Egger carried inextinguishably within him: a pain that, after the brief touch of a fold of fabric, had sunk into the flesh of his upper arm, his shoulder, his breast, finally settling somewhere in the region of his heart. It was a very subtle pain, yet it was more profound than any Egger had encountered in his life so far, including Kranzstocker's blows with the hazel rod.

Her name was Marie, and Egger thought it the most beautiful name in the world. She had appeared in the valley a few months earlier, looking for work, with trodden-down shoes and dusty hair. It was good timing, as the innkeeper had told his maid to go to the devil just a few days before, for unexpectedly falling pregnant. 'Show me your hands!' he said to Marie. He inspected the calluses on her fingers with a satisfied nod and offered her the vacant position. From then on she served the guests and made the beds in the handful of rooms furnished for seasonal workers. She assumed responsibility for the chickens, helped out in the garden and in the kitchen, slaughtered animals and emptied the guests' toilet. She never complained, and she wasn't vain or squeamish. 'You keep your hands off her!' said the innkeeper, stabbing Egger's chest with a forefinger that gleamed with freshly rendered lard. 'Marie's a girl for work, not love, understood?'

'Understood,' said Egger, and felt again the subtle pain near his heart. There are no lies before God, he thought, but there are before an innkeeper.

He waited for her after church on Sunday. She was wearing a white dress and had a little white hat on her head. Although this little hat looked very pretty, Egger thought perhaps it was slightly too small. He was reminded of the rootstocks that protruded darkly here and there from the forest floor and on which, from time to time, a single white lily would bloom, like a miracle. But perhaps the little hat was just right; Egger didn't know. He had no idea about these things. His experiences of women were limited to church services, during which he would sit in the very back row of the chapel listening to their high, clear voices, practically anaesthetized by the Sunday scent wafting from hair that had been washed with soap and rubbed with lavender.

'I would like . . .' he said roughly, and broke off in mid-sentence, having suddenly forgotten what it was he actually wanted to say. They stood for a while in silence in the shadow of the chapel. She looked tired. Her face still seemed veiled by the twilight of the church's interior. A yellow speck of pollen clung to her left eyebrow, quivering in the breeze. Suddenly she smiled at him. 'It's getting chilly,' she said. 'Maybe we could walk in the sun for a bit.'

They walked side by side along the forest path that wound up from behind the chapel to the Harzerkogl. A little stream trickled in the grass and the treetops rustled above them. Everywhere in the undergrowth they could hear the chirping of robins, but whenever they came too close the birds fell silent. They reached a clearing and stopped. High above their heads a falcon hung motionless. Suddenly it flapped its wings and tipped sideways; it seemed simply to fall from the sky and vanish from their sight. Marie picked some flowers and Egger hurled a stone the size of a head into the undergrowth, on impulse, just because he had the inclination and the strength to do it. As they were crossing a rotten footbridge on the way back she grasped his forearm. Her hand was rough and warm like a piece of sunlit wood. Egger would have liked to place it against his cheek and simply stop and stand there. Instead he took a big step and walked swiftly on. 'Be very careful,' he said, without turning to look at her. 'You can easily twist an ankle on this ground.'

They met every Sunday, and sometimes, later on, during the week as well. As a small child, climbing over a rickety wooden fence, she had fallen into the pigsty and been bitten by a startled mother sow. Ever since, she had had a bright red scar across the nape of her neck, about twenty centimetres long and shaped like a crescent moon. It didn't bother Egger. Scars are like years, he said: one follows another and it's all of them together that make a person who they are. Marie, for her part, wasn't bothered by his crooked leg. At least, she didn't say anything. She never mentioned his limp, not with so much as a word. But then the two of them didn't talk much. They walked alongside each other, contemplating their shadows on the ground before them, or sat on a rock somewhere and gazed across the valley.

One afternoon towards the end of August he took her up to his plot of land. He bent down, opened the little wooden gate and stood back for her to enter. He still had to paint the cabin, he said; wind and damp gnawed through wood before you knew it, you see, and then you could forget all about being snug. Over there he'd planted a few vegetables, celery for example, already almost as high as your head. The sun shone more brightly up here than down in the valley, you see. Which wasn't just good for the plants; it warmed the bones and the spirit, too. Not to mention the view, of course, said Egger, with a sweep of his arm; you could see right across the whole region, even further when the weather was good. He wanted to paint inside as well, he explained to her, with masonry paint. You had to dilute it with fresh milk instead of water, of course, to make it last. And the kitchen still needed to be properly equipped, but at least the essentials were already there, pots, plates, cutlery and things, and when he had a chance he'd sand down the frying pans as well. He wouldn't need a shed, incidentally, because he didn't have either the space or time for cattle; after all, he didn't want to be a farmer. Being a farmer meant spending your whole life crawling around on your clod of land with your eyes lowered, scratching at the earth. His kind of man needed to lift up his eyes and look as far as possible beyond his own small, limited patch of ground.

In later life Egger couldn't remember ever having talked as much as he did the day Marie first visited his cabin. The words simply tumbled out of him and he listened to them in astonishment as they lined up, seemingly of their own accord, to create a meaning that became apparent to him with surprising clarity only after he had spoken them.

As they descended the narrow, winding path to the valley, Egger fell silent again. He felt strange and a little embarrassed, without knowing why. They stopped for a while at a bend in the path, sat in the grass and leaned their backs against the trunk of a fallen beech. The wood had stored the warmth of the last days of summer and smelled of dry moss and resin. All around them the moun-taintops rose up into the clear sky. Marie thought they looked as if they were made of porcelain, and although Egger had never seen porcelain in his life he agreed with her. You'd have to be careful walking there, he said; one false step and the whole landscape might crack, or shatter straight away into thousands of tiny landscape-splinters. Marie laughed. 'That sounds funny,' she said.

'Yes,' said Egger. Then he bowed his head, not knowing what to do next. He would have liked to stand up, grab a rock and fling it somewhere at random, as high and as far as possible. Suddenly he felt her shoulder against his shoulder. He raised his head and said, 'I can't stand it any longer!' He turned towards her, took her face in both hands and kissed her.

'Goodness,' she said. 'Aren't you strong!'

'Sorry,' he said, alarmed, and drew back his hands.

'It was nice, though,' she said.

'Even though it hurt?'

'Yes,' she said. 'Very nice.'

He took her face in his hands once more, this time as gently as you would cradle a hen's egg or a newly hatched chick.

'That's right,' she said, and closed her eyes.

He would have liked to ask for her hand that very day, or the following day at the latest, but he had no idea how to go about it. For nights on end he sat in front of his house on the threshold he had built, staring at the moonlit grass at his feet while his thoughts revolved around his own inadequacies. He wasn't a farmer, and he didn't want to be one. But he wasn't a craftsman either, or a woodsman, or a herdsman. In truth, he made his living as a kind of labourer, a hired hand for all seasons and occasions. A man like that was good for pretty much anything, but not as a prospective husband. Women expected more from a husband-to-be: this much Egger thought he did understand about them. If it were up to him he would spend the rest of his life sitting beside a path somewhere, hand in hand with Marie, leaning against a resinous tree trunk. But it wasn't just up to him now. He knew his responsibilities in this world. He wanted to protect Marie and take care of her. A man needed to lift up his eyes and look as far as possible beyond his own small, limited patch of ground. That was what he had told her, and that was what he intended to do.

Egger paid a visit to the camp of Bittermann & Sons, which by now had expanded to cover the whole of the sloping meadow on the other side of the valley, and had more inhabitants than the village itself. He asked his way to the hut of the general manager, who was responsible for hiring new workers, and entered his office with unaccustomed hesitancy: he was afraid his rough boots might damage the carpet, which covered practically the whole of the floor and muffled his steps as if he were walking on moss. The general manager was a heavy man whose bald, scarred head was fringed with a crown of short-cropped hair. He was sitting behind a black wooden desk wearing a leather jacket lined with sheepskin, despite the warmth in the room. He was poring over a stack of files and seemed not to have noticed Egger's entrance, but just as Egger was about to make some sort of noise to attract his attention he unexpectedly raised his head.

'You limp,' he said. 'We can't use someone like you.'

'There's no better worker around here than me,' Egger answered. 'I'm strong. I can do anything. I'll do anything.'

'But you limp.'

'In the valley, maybe,' said Egger. 'On the mountain I'm the only one who walks upright.'

The general manager slowly leaned back. Silence filled the room, settling like a dark veil over Egger's heart. He stared at the whitewashed wall and for a moment he could no longer remember why he had come here at all. The manager sighed. He raised his hand and made a gesture as if trying to erase Egger from his field of vision. Then he said, 'Welcome to Bittermann & Sons. No alcohol, no whoring, no unions. Start tomorrow morning, half-past five!'

———

Egger helped to cut timber and erect the massive iron girders that threaded their way at fifty-metre intervals along a dead straight line, further and further up the mountain. Each one towered several metres over the congregational chapel, the highest building in the village. He carried iron, wood and cement up the hillside and back down again. He dug foundation trenches in the forest floor and drilled holes in the rock as big as an arm for the chief blaster to lay his sticks of dynamite. During the blasting he squatted at a safe distance with the others on the tree trunks that lay to the left and right of the wide forest aisle. They covered their ears and felt the detonations, which made the mountain tremble beneath their backsides. Because he knew the area like practically no one else, and also had an excellent head for heights, he was usually sent on ahead and was first to arrive at the drill site. He scrambled over scree, climbed between rocks, and hung on the steep mountain face secured only by a thin rope, his gaze fixed on the small cloud of dust his drill raised in front of his face. Egger liked working on the rock. The air up here was cool and clear, and sometimes he heard the scream of a golden eagle, or saw its shadow glide noiselessly across the rock. He often thought of

Marie. Of her warm, rough hand, and her scar, the curve of which he traced over and over again in his mind's eye.

In the autumn Egger was overcome with restlessness. He believed the time had finally come for him to ask Marie for her hand, but he still had no idea how to go about it. He sat on his doorstep in the evenings and surrendered himself to hazy ideas and dreams. Of course, he thought, his proposal could not just be any old proposal. It had to be one that somehow epitomized the magnitude of his love and would engrave itself for ever on Marie's memory and heart. Something in writing, he thought; but he wrote even more seldom than he spoke, which meant almost never. On top of which, in his opinion, a letter wasn't really up to the task. How were all his thoughts and feelings in their profusion supposed to fit onto a single sheet of paper? Ideally he would have liked to inscribe his love on the mountain, in huge letters, visible for miles around to everyone in the valley. He explained his problem to his colleague Thomas Mattl, who was pulling recalcitrant rootstocks out of the earth with him at the edge of the forest aisle. Mattl was an experienced lumberjack and one of the company's longest-serving employees. For almost thirty years he had been travelling with different teams throughout the mountain regions, clearing the forests in the name of progress and planting iron girders or concrete pillars into the ground. Despite his age, and the pains that he said had sunk their teeth into his lower back like a pack of rabid dogs, he was light on his feet and moved nimbly through the undergrowth. Perhaps there really was a way of inscribing something on the mountain, said Mattl, running his hand over his bearded face: with the devil's ink, which was to say, with fire. In his youth he had spent a couple of summers chopping wood for bridges in the north. There he had encountered the ancient tradition of the Sacred Heart Fires, huge fire pictures that were lit on the summer solstice, illuminating the mountain by night. If you could draw with fire, he said, you could write with it, too. Some kind of proposal for this Marie, for example. Three, four words, no more than that, of course, you couldn't do more than that. *Will you have me?* or *Come, sweetheart*; whatever it is women like to hear.

'That could work,' Mattl added thoughtfully. Then he reached behind his head and pulled out a slender, budding twig that had caught in his collar. He bit off the little white buds one by one and sucked them like sweets.

'Yes,' Egger nodded. 'That could work.'

Two weeks later, in the late afternoon of the first Sunday in October, seventeen of the most reliable men in Egger's team were clambering around in the scree above the Adlerkante. They were laying out, according to Mattl's hoarsely barked instructions, two hundred and fifty little cloth bags, filled with sawdust and soaked in paraffin, each weighing one and a half kilograms, at approximately two-metre intervals along a line marked out with hemp ropes. A few days earlier Egger had gathered the men in the canteen tent after work to explain his plans and per-suade them to play a part. 'You'll get seventy groschen and a quarter-litre of Krauterer,' he said, looking into the men's dirty faces one by one. Over the preceding weeks he had saved the money from his wages, collecting the coins in a little candle-box which he had deposited in a hole in the ground beneath his threshold.

'We want eighty groschen and half a litre!' said a black-haired engine fitter, who had joined the firm from Lombardy just a couple of weeks earlier and, thanks to his pressure-cooker temperament, had quickly acquired a certain authority within the team.

'Ninety groschen and no Krauterer,' countered Egger.

'There has to be Krauterer.'

'Sixty groschen and half a litre.'

'Done!' shouted the black-haired man, and banged his fist on the table to confirm the deal.

Thomas Mattl spent most of the time sitting on a spur of rock, keeping an eye on what the men were doing. Under no circumstances should the bags be more than two metres apart, otherwise there would be gaps in the writing. 'We can't let love perish because of a gap in a letter, you fool,' he shouted, flinging a fist-sized stone in the direction of a young scaffolder whose spaces had come out slightly too big.

All the bags were laid out just in time for sunset. Night was settling over the mountains and Mattl crawled down from his rock towards the first bag of the first letter. He surveyed the hillside and the men spread out evenly across it. Then he slapped the dust off his trousers, fished a box of matches out of his trouser pocket and ignited a stick wrapped in paraffin-soaked rags that was planted in the ground in front of him. He took the torch, brandished it above his head, and gave the clearest, loudest whoop he had ever come out with in his life. Almost simultaneously sixteen torches flared across the scree and the men began to run along the lines as fast as they could, igniting the bags one after another. Mattl chuckled quietly. He thought with pleasure of the schnapps that awaited him, while at the back of his neck he sensed the cool breath of the night as it descended ever deeper over the mountains.

At this precise moment, down in the valley, Andreas Egger was putting his arm around Marie's shoulders. They had arranged to meet at sunset on the tree stump beside the old footbridge, and to Egger's relief she had arrived on time. She was wearing a pale linen dress and her hair smelled of soap, hay, and also, Egger thought, a little of roast pork. He spread his jacket over the tree stump and indicated for her to sit. He wanted to show her something, he said, something she might never forget. 'Something nice?' asked Marie. 'Could be,' he said. They sat beside each other and watched in silence as the sun disappeared behind the mountains. Egger heard his own heart pounding. For a moment it seemed to him to be beating not within his breast but in the tree stump beneath him, as if the mouldy wood had awakened to new life. Then they heard Thomas Mattl's whoop far away in the distance, and Egger pointed out into the darkness. 'Look,' he said. A second later sixteen lights flickered high up on the opposite side of the valley, moving in every direction like a swarm of fireflies. As they moved, the lights seemed to lose glowing drops which joined up, one by one, to form curving lines. Egger felt Marie's body next to his. He put his arm around her shoulders and heard her quiet breathing. On the other side of the valley the glowing lines swooped across the hillside in arc after arc, or closed in rounded shapes. Right at the end a single dot lit up above the I on the top right, and Egger knew that old Mattl himself had clambered across the scree to ignite the last bag of paraffin. FOR YOU, MARIE stood inscribed on the mountain in huge, flickering letters, visible for miles around to everyone in the valley. The 'M' was rather crooked, and there was a piece missing, too, so that it looked as if someone had pulled it apart in the middle. At least two of the bags had apparently failed to catch fire, or hadn't been set at all. Egger took a deep breath: then he turned to Marie and tried to make out her face in the darkness.

'Will you be my wife?' he asked.

'Yes,' she whispered, so quietly he wasn't sure he'd understood her correctly.

'Will you, Marie?' he asked again.

'Yes, I will,' she said, in a firm voice, and Egger felt as if he was about to keel backwards off the tree stump; but he stayed on his seat. They embraced, and when at last they let each other go the fires on the mountain had gone out.

Egger's nights were no longer lonely now. In bed beside him lay his quietly breathing wife. Sometimes he would contemplate the outline of her body beneath the blanket: although over the weeks he had got to know it better and better, it still seemed to him like an incomprehensible miracle. Officially, he was now thirty-three years old, and he knew his responsibilities. He would protect Marie and take care of her: that was what he had told himself, and that was what he wanted to do. And that was why, one Monday morning, he came once again to stand in front of the general manager's desk in his cabin. 'I want more work,' he said, turning his woollen hat in his hands.

The general manager raised his head and gave him a weary look. 'No one wants more work.'

'I do. Because I'm going to have a family.'

'So you want more money, not more work.'

'If that's how you see it, I expect that's right.'

'Yes, I think that is how I see it. How much do you earn now?'

'Sixty groschen an hour.'

The general manager leaned back and gazed out of the window, where the white tip of the Hahnenzinne stood out behind a layer of dust. Slowly he stroked a hand across his bald head. Then he exhaled heavily and looked Egger in the eyes. 'You can have eighty, but I want you to work your backside off for every single groschen. Will you do that?'

Egger nodded and the general manager sighed. Then he said something that, although he didn't understand it at the time, Egger was to remember all his life: 'You can buy a man's hours off him, you can steal his days from him, or you can rob him of his whole life, but no one can take away from any man so much as a single moment. That's the way it is. Now leave me in peace!'

* * *

The Bittermann & Sons construction teams had now worked their way well past the tree line, leaving behind them a scar through the forest one and a half kilometres long and up to thirty metres wide in places. It was only about another four hundred metres to the planned top station just below the Karleitner peak, but the terrain was steep and inaccessible. The final stretch had to span an almost perpendicular wall capped with an overhanging rock known to the locals, on account of its shape, as the Giant's Skull. For many days Egger hung directly beneath the chin of the Giant's Skull, boring holes in the granite and twisting in mounting screws the size of his forearm, which would later support a long metal ladder for the maintenance technicians. He thought with secret pride of the men who would one day climb up and down this ladder, never knowing that they owed their lives entirely to him and his dexterity. During the short breaks he took to catch his breath he squatted on a ledge of rock and looked out over the valley. For some weeks now they had been gravelling and tarring the old road, and through the foggy vapour he could make out the silhouettes of men working the hot asphalt with pickaxes and shovels, so distant that they seemed to be-doing so in utter silence.

In winter Egger was one of the few workers who remained on the company payroll. Along with a handful of other men, including Thomas Mattl, whose lifelong forestry experience had proven extremely useful to the company, he continued to widen the aisle and clear it of stones, waste wood and rootstocks. Often they would be standing up to their hips in snow, hacking a root out of the frozen ground, while the wind blew flakes of ice in their faces like grains of shot until their skin began to bleed. While working they spoke only when necessary, and in their lunch breaks they would sit in silence beneath a snow-covered fir tree, toasting their breadsticks over the fire. They crawled after each other through the brush, or sat in the lee of a rock during a storm, blowing on hands lacerated with cold. They were like animals, Egger thought; they crawled over the earth, relieved themselves behind the nearest tree, and were so filthy they could barely be distinguished from their surroundings. Often, too, he thought of Marie, who was waiting for him at home. He was no longer alone, and although this feeling was still an unaccustomed one, it warmed him more than the fire into whose embers he thrust his rock-hard, frozen boots.

In the spring, after the onset of the snowmelt, when a mysterious dripping and burbling had begun all over the forest, there was an accident in Egger's team. They were working on a Swiss stone pine that had buckled under the weight of the snow, when the tension in the wood released itself with a sharp crack. A splinter the height of a man sprang from the trunk, ripping off the young lumberjack Gustl Grollerer's right arm, which, as bad luck would have it, he had raised high above his head again ready for the next blow of the axe. Grollerer collapsed to the ground and stared at his arm. It lay on the forest floor two metres away, its fingers still gripping the hatchet. For a moment a strange silence settled over the scene, as if the whole forest had frozen and were holding its breath. In the end it was Thomas Mattl who was first to move. 'Jesus,' he said, 'that looks bad.' He went to the toolbox, fetched a wire loop for scraping off bark and, using all his strength, pulled it tight around the stump of Grollerer's arm, which was gushing dark blood. Grollerer bellowed and thrashed from side to side, then lay still, unconscious.

'We'll soon fix this,' said Mattl, wrapping his handkerchief around the wound. 'Nobody bleeds to death that quickly!' One of the men suggested cutting branches to make a stretcher. Another started to rub the stump with a handful of forest herbs, but was quickly pushed aside. Eventually they agreed that it would be best to carry the injured man down to the village as he was, strap him to the back of a diesel truck and drive him to hospital. The machine fitter from Lombardy lifted Grollerer off the ground and laid him across his shoulders like a limp sack. A brief discussion ensued as to what should happen to the arm. Some suggested they should pack it up and take it with them: perhaps the doctors could sew it back on. Others contradicted them: not even the most fiendish of doctors had ever sewn an entire arm back on, and even if they somehow managed to do such a thing it would just hang there at Grollerer's side for the rest of his life, slack and ugly and making things difficult for him. It was Grollerer himself who put an end to the discussion when he regained consciousness, lifted his head from the fitter's shoulder and said: 'Bury my arm in the forest. Maybe a blackcurrant bush will grow out of it!'

While the other men headed down to the village with Gustl Grollerer, now an ex-lumberjack, Egger and Thomas Mattl stayed behind at the scene of the accident to bury the arm. The leaves and earth it lay on were dark with blood and its fingers felt waxen and cold as they prised them from the handle of the axe. A little jet-black long-horned beetle was sitting on the tip of the index finger. Mattl held the stiff arm out in front of him and examined it with narrowed eyes. 'It's strange,' he said. 'A moment ago this was still part of Grollerer. Now it's dead and worth not much more than a rotten branch. What do you reckon – is Grollerer still Grollerer now?'

Egger shrugged his shoulders. 'Why not? He's Grollerer, with only one arm.'

'What if the tree had ripped off both arms?'

'Then too. He'd still be Grollerer.'

'And say it had ripped away both arms, both legs, and half his head?'

Egger considered. 'He'd probably still be Grollerer, even then . . . somehow.' Suddenly he was no longer quite so sure.

Thomas Mattl sighed. He placed the arm gently on the toolbox and together, with a couple of cuts of the spade, they dug a hole in the ground. In the meantime the forest had begun to breathe again and birds were singing over their heads. It had been a chilly day, but now the blanket of clouds dispersed and sunlight fell in shimmering bundles through the canopy of leaves, making the earth muddy and soft. They placed the arm in its little grave and shovelled it in. The fingers were last to disappear. For a moment they stuck up out of the earth like fat mealworms, then they were gone. Mattl pulled out his little pouch of tobacco and filled his pipe, which he had carved himself out of plum wood.

'It's a messy business, dying,' he said. 'As time goes on there's just less and less of you. It happens quickly for some; for others it can drag on. Starting from birth you keep losing one thing after another: first a finger, then an arm, first a tooth, then a whole set of teeth, first one memory, then all your memory, and so on and so forth, until one day there's nothing left. Then they chuck what's left of you in a hole and shovel it in and that's your lot.'

'And there will be a cold,' said Egger. 'A cold that gnaws the soul.' The old man looked at him. Then he twisted his mouth and spat just past the stem of his pipe at the treacherous splinter of pine, its edges sticky with Grollerer's blood. 'Rubbish. There won't be anything, no cold and certainly no soul. Dead is dead and that's that. There's nothing after that – no God, either. Because if there were a God, his heavenly kingdom wouldn't be so bloody far away!'

Thomas Mattl was taken from this world nine years later, almost to the day. All his life he had hoped he would die on the job, but it happened differently. While bathing in the only bathtub in the camp, a battered monstrosity of galvanized iron that one of the cooks rented out to the workers for a small sum, Thomas Mattl fell asleep. When he woke the water was icy, and he caught a cold from which he never recovered. For several nights he lay sweating on his pallet, babbling incoherently, about either his long-dead mother or 'bloodsucking forest demons'. Then one morning he got up and declared that he was now well and wanted to go to work. He pulled on his trousers, stepped outside the door, craned his head towards the sun and fell down dead. He was buried next to the village cemetery, in the steeply sloping meadow the company had purchased from the local authority. Virtually all the employees who were able to gathered there to say goodbye, and listened to the short funeral address that one of the foremen had cobbled together, which talked about the hard work on the mountain and Mattl's pure soul.

Thomas Mattl was one of an official total of thirty-seven men who died while working for Bittermann & Sons, up until the firm went bankrupt in 1946. In truth, however, many more gave their lives for the cable-car industry, which expanded ever faster from the 1930s on. 'For every gondola someone goes underground,' Mattl had said in one of his final nights. By then, though, the other men were no longer taking him all that seriously; they thought the fever had already burned the last vestiges of his wits from his brain.

And so Andreas Egger's first year with Bittermann & Sons came to an end, and the 1st Wendenkogler Aerial Cable Car (this was its official title, though only the mayor and the tourists ever used it – the locals just called it Blue Liesl on account of its two lightning-blue cabins, which also, owing to their rather flat front sections, bore a certain resemblance to the mayor's wife) was inaugurated in a big opening ceremony at the top station. A whole host of fashionable people from beyond the valley stood on the platform freezing in thin suits and even thinner dresses, and the priest shouted his blessing into the wind with his cassock flapping around his body like the dishevelled plumage of a jackdaw. Egger stood amid his colleagues, who had spread out across the mountain below the Giant's Skull, and every time he saw the people clapping up there on the platform he threw his arms into the air and let out a cheer of enthusiasm. In his heart there was a curious sensation of expansiveness and pride. He felt that he was part of something big, something that far exceeded his own powers (including the power of his imagination), and which he thought he could see would spell progress, not just for life in the valley but also, somehow, for the whole of humankind. Ever since the test ride a few days earlier, when Blue Liesl had wobbled her way to the top, juddering cautiously but without major mishap, the mountains seemed to have forfeited something of their enduring might. And more cable cars would follow. The company had extended the contracts of almost all its workers and presented plans to build a total of fifteen aerial cable cars, including a hair-raising construction that proposed to transport passengers with rucksacks and skis in free-floating wooden chairs instead of carriages. Egger thought this a rather ridiculous idea, but he secretly admired the engineers who squeezed such fantastical things out of their heads, and for whom neither snowstorms nor the heat of summer could cloud either their optimism or the shine on their immaculately polished shoes.

* * *

Half a lifetime or almost four decades later, in the summer of 1972, Egger stood on the same spot watching the shining silver gondolas of what was once Blue Liesl glide swiftly along, high above his head, accompanied by an almost inaudible buzzing. Up on the platform the cabin doors opened with a drawn-out hiss and discharged a crowd of day-trippers who streamed off in all directions, dispersing like bright insects over the mountain. These people who clambered about so recklessly on the scree annoyed Egger. They seemed to be constantly searching for some sort of hidden miracle. He would have liked to plant himself in their way and give them a piece of his mind, but he didn't really know what exactly he would reproach them for. Secretly – this much at least he could admit to himself – he envied them. He saw them jumping over the rocks in trainers and shorts, putting their children on their shoulders and smiling into their cameras, whereas he was an old man, good for nothing any more and glad still to be able to move about more or less upright. He had already been so long in the world: he had seen it change and seem to spin faster with every passing year, and he felt like a remnant from some long-buried time, a thorny weed still stretching up, for as long as it possibly could, towards the sun.

* * *

The weeks and months after the opening ceremony at the top station were the happiest of Andreas Egger's life. He saw himself as a small but not unimportant cog in a gigantic machine called Progress, and sometimes, before falling asleep, he would picture himself sitting in the belly of this machine as it ploughed inexorably through forests and mountains, contributing, with the heat and sweat of his brow, to its ongoing advance. He had taken the words *with the heat and sweat of his brow* from a tattered magazine Marie had found under one of the benches in the inn, and from which she would sometimes read to him in the evenings. In addition to all kinds of ideas about urban fashion, gardening, the keeping of pets and general morality, the magazine also contained a story. It was about an impoverished Russian nobleman who drove his lover, a peasant's daughter blessed with strange gifts, across half of Russia one winter to rescue her from persecution by some fanatically religious village elders, including her own father, and bring her to safety. The story ended tragically, but it contained a large number of so-called *romantic scenes* which Marie read out with an almost imperceptible tremor in her voice, and which evoked in Egger a strange mixture of disgust and fascination. He listened to the words coming out of Marie's mouth and sensed a heat slowly spreading beneath his blanket which, it seemed to him, would soon fill the entire cabin. Whenever the impoverished nobleman and the peasant's daughter dashed across the snow-covered steppe in their carriage, at their backs the clattering of horses and the furious cries of their pursuers, and the terrified girl threw herself into the count's arms, brushing his cheek as she did so with the seam of a dress already dirty from the journey, Egger could stand it no longer. He would kick away his blanket and stare with inflamed eyes into the flickering gloom beneath the roof beams. Then Marie would place the magazine carefully under the bed and blow out the candle. 'Come,' she whispered in the darkness, and Egger obeyed.

At the end of March 1935, Egger and Marie were sitting on the threshold after sunset, looking out over the valley. It had snowed a lot in the last few weeks, but for two days now a sudden warm spell had been announcing the arrival of spring: all around the snow was melting, and already during the day the baby swallows' beaks were peeping out over the edge of their nest under the eaves. From morning till night the adult swallows flew to their young with worms and insects in their beaks, and Egger commented that 'all that bird shit would be enough to lay a new foundation'. But Marie liked the birds; she thought of them as fluttering good-luck charms keeping evil away from the house, so he resigned himself to the mess and the nest was allowed to stay.

Egger's gaze travelled all across the village and the opposite side of the valley. In many houses the windows were already lit up. The valley had had electricity for a while now and some days, here or there, an old farmer could be seen sitting before a lamp in his room and staring in astonishment into its bright glow. The lights were already on in the workers' camp, too, and smoke was rising almost vertically from narrow iron pipes into the cloudy evening sky. From a distance it looked as if the clouds were attached to the roofs by thin threads, suspended over the valley like huge, shapeless balloons. Blue Liesl's cabins were still, and Egger thought of the two maintenance engineers who right at this moment were crawling around the engine room with their little cans of oil, lubricating the machinery. Another cable car had already been completed, and they had started to cut an aisle in the forest in the neighbouring valley for a third, longer and wider than the first two put together. Egger looked at his steep, snow-covered land spread out before him. He felt a small, warm wave of contentment well up inside, and would have liked to leap to his feet and shout out his happiness to the world, but Marie was sitting there so quiet and still that he too remained seated.

'Maybe we can have some more vegetables,' he said. 'I could extend the garden. Behind the house, I mean. Potatoes, onions and things.'

'Yes, that's not a bad idea, Andreas,' she said. Egger looked at her. He couldn't recall her ever having addressed him by name. It was the first time, and it felt strange. She passed the back of her hand across her brow and he looked away again. 'We'll have to see whether all that can grow in soil like this,' he said, poking the tip of his shoe into the frozen earth.

'Something's going to grow. And it's going to be something wonderful,' she said. Egger looked at her again. She was leaning back slightly, and her face was barely visible in the shadow of the doorway. All he could make out were her eyes, two shining drops in the darkness.

'Why are you looking like that?' he asked quietly. Suddenly he felt uneasy, sitting there beside this woman who was at the same time both so familiar to him and so alien. She leaned forward a little and placed her hands in her lap. They seemed to him unusually delicate and white. Impossible that just a few hours ago they had been splitting firewood with an axe. He stretched out his arm and touched Marie's shoulder, and although he was still looking at the white hands in her lap, he knew that she was smiling.

In the night Egger was woken by a peculiar noise. It was no more than an intimation, a soft whisper stealing around the walls. He lay in the dark and listened. He felt the warmth of his wife beside him and heard the quiet sounds of her breathing. Eventually he got up and went outside. The warm föhn wind buffeted against him, almost wrenching the door out of his hand. Black clouds were racing across the night sky, a pale, shapeless moon flickering between them. Egger trudged a little way up the field. The snow was heavy and wet and the meltwater was burbling all around. He thought about the vegetables and about all the other things he needed to do. The soil didn't yield much, but it would be enough. They could have a goat or perhaps even a cow, he thought, for the milk. He stopped. Somewhere way up high he heard a sound, as if something deep inside the mountain were splitting with a sigh. Then he heard a deep, swelling rumble and a moment later the ground beneath his feet began to tremble. Suddenly he was cold. Within seconds the rumbling had increased to a high, piercing note. Egger stood stock-still and heard the mountain start to sing. Then he saw something big and black hurtle silently past about twenty metres away and before he had even grasped that it was a tree trunk he began to run. He ran back through the deep snow towards the house, calling to Marie, but an instant later something seized him and lifted him up. He felt himself being carried away and the last thing he saw before a dark wave engulfed him was his legs, sticking up above him into the sky as if disconnected from the rest of his body.

When Egger came to, the clouds had disappeared and in the night sky the moon was a radiant white. All around the mountains soared up in its light; their icy crests looked as if they had been punched from a sheet of metal, their sharpness and clarity seeming to cut into the sky. Egger was lying on his back at an angle. He could move his head and arms, but his legs were buried up to the hips in snow.

He began to dig. Using both hands he shovelled and scratched his legs out of the snow and when he had freed them he saw them lying there, stunned, as cold and alien as two planks of wood. He pounded his thighs with his fists. 'Don't abandon me now,' he said, and finally gave a hoarse laugh as pain shot into them along with the blood. He tried to stand, but immediately buckled again. He cursed his good-for-nothing legs and cursed his whole body, weaker than that of a little child. 'Come on, up you get!' he said to himself, and when he tried again he managed it, and stood. The landscape had changed. The avalanche had buried trees and rocks beneath it and levelled the ground. The deep snow lay like a vast blanket in the moonlight. He tried to get his bearings from the mountains. As far as he could tell, he was about three hundred metres below his cabin, which must be up there behind the mound of piled-up snow. He set off. The going was slower than he had thought: the avalanche snow was unpredictable, rock-hard in one place as if fused with the bedrock, soft and powdery as icing sugar just two steps further on. The pain was bad. He was particularly worried about his good leg. It felt as if there was an iron thorn stuck in his thigh, boring deeper and deeper into his flesh with every step he took. He thought of the young swal-lows. Hopefully the shock wave hadn't got them. The nest was in a well-protected spot, though, and he had built the roof frame sturdy. Still, he would need to strengthen the crossbeams underneath; he would weigh the roof down with stones and protect the back with a supporting wall of interlocking rock fragments that he would work deep into the slope. 'But the stones must be flat!' he said aloud to himself. He stopped for a moment and listened, but there was hardly a sound. The föhn wind had vanished, leaving only a delicate breeze that tingled on the skin. He walked on. The world around him was silent and dead. For a moment he had the feeling that he was the last person on earth, or at least the last person in the valley. He laughed. 'What nonsense,' he said, and walked on. The last stretch before the mound of snow was steep and he had to crawl on all fours. Beneath his fingers the snow was crumbly and seemed to him curiously warm. Strangely, the pain in his legs had now vanished, but the cold still sat deep in his bones, and they felt as light and brittle as glass. 'I'm nearly there,' he said to himself or to Marie or to anyone, but even as he did so he knew there was no longer anyone to hear him, and when he heaved his body up over the crest of the hill he uttered a loud sob. He knelt in the snow and surveyed the moonlit expanse on which his house had stood. He shouted his wife's name into the silence: 'Marie! Marie!' He stood up and walked aimlessly around his piece of land. Beneath a knee-deep layer of powder the snow was hard and smooth, as if pressed by a roller. Shingles, stones and broken wood lay scattered all around. He recognized the iron ring of his rain barrel and, beside it, one of his boots. In one slightly elevated spot a piece of the chimney stuck up out of the ground. Egger went on a couple of steps to where he guessed the entrance must be. He fell on his knees and began to dig. He dug until his hands bled and the snow turned dark beneath him. An hour later, when he had got down about one and a half metres, he felt beneath his raw fingertips, as if embedded in cement, a roof beam that the avalanche had torn away, and stopped digging. He sat back and stared up into the night sky. Then he fell forward and laid his face in the blood-drenched snow.

It was weeks before the fragments of individual accounts were pieced together and the valley dwellers were able to put what had happened that night into some kind of order in their minds. The avalanche had come at two thirty in the morning. A huge lump of snow had detached itself from a cornice about fifty metres below the Almerspitze and had plunged down the mountain with considerable force. As the terrain where it broke off was almost vertical, the avalanche swiftly gained speed, leaving a trail of devastation as it hurtled down into the valley. The mass of snow thundered past just behind the village and all the way across to the far side of the valley, where it triggered a smaller, secondary avalanche whose northern fringes reached as far as the Bittermann & Sons camp, finally coming to a standstill just an arm's length from Thomas Mattl's old bathtub. The avalanche uprooted the forest and swept it along with it, leaving a deep trough that extended all the way to the hillock beside the village pond. The villagers reported hearing a muffled detonation followed by a rushing or roaring sound, like the galloping of an enormous herd of cattle descending the mountain and rapidly approaching the village. The shock wave made windows tremble, and everywhere Madonna figurines and crucifixes fell from the walls. People fled their houses and ran out into the street, ducking their heads beneath a cloud of snow dust that seemed to swallow the stars. They gathered in front of the chapel, and the avalanche's dying rumbles were accompanied by a whispered chorus of women praying. Slowly the snow cloud settled, coating everything in a fine white layer. A deathly silence lay over the valley and the inhabitants knew that it was over.

The damage was devastating, far worse even than the great avalanche of 1873, which a couple of the oldest villagers thought they still remembered: at the Ogfreiner farm sixteen crosses carved into the family altar bore silent witness to its sixteen buried souls. This time four farms, two large haystacks and the mayor's little mill in the mountain stream as well as five workers' cabins and one of the camp latrines were completely destroyed, or at least substantially damaged. Nineteen cows, twenty-eight pigs, countless chickens and the only six sheep in the village all met their deaths. Their cadavers were dragged out of the snow by tractors or with bare hands and burned with the wooden debris that couldn't be reused. The stench of burnt flesh hung in the air for days and masked the smell of spring, which had now definitely arrived, melting the snow masses and revealing the full extent of the disaster. Nonetheless, on Sunday the villagers gathered together in the chapel and thanked the Lord for his goodness, for only divine mercy could explain why the avalanche had taken the lives of no more than three people: the venerable old farming couple Simon and Hedwig Jonasser, whose house had been completely encased in snow and who were found, after rescuers had worked their way through to the bedroom, lying in bed in each other's arms, cheek to cheek, asphyxiated; and the maid from the guesthouse, Marie Reisenbacher, Andreas Egger's young bride.

The men from a rescue team hastily assembled on the night of the disaster found Egger's cabin swallowed by the snow and Egger himself lying doubled up beside a hole he had dug in the snow with his bare hands. They told him afterwards that he didn't stir as they approached the scene, and none of them would have bet so much as a groschen that there was any life left in that dark heap of a man. Egger couldn't remember a single detail of his actual rescue, but the dreamlike image of torches emerging from the darkness of the night and moving slowly towards him, wavering like ghosts, remained with him till the day he died.

Marie's body was recovered, laid out in the chapel beside the Jonassers, and buried in the parish cemetery. The funeral took place in radiant sunshine with the first bumblebees buzzing over the turned earth. Egger sat on a stool, sick and rigid with sorrow, accepting people's condolences. He didn't understand what they were saying to him, and their hands felt as if they were foreign objects being given to him to hold.

In the weeks that followed, Egger found accommodation at the Golden Goat. Most of the time he lay in bed in a tiny room behind the laundry which the innkeeper had offered for him to use. His broken legs took a long time to heal. The bonesetter Alois Klammerer had died years earlier (cancer ate away his palate, half his jaw and the side of his face so that by the end you could see his teeth through his open cheek as if through a window), so they had to call in the young local doctor, who had moved to the village just last season and was making a living primarily from the sprained, twisted or broken limbs of the tourists who came in ever-increasing numbers for hiking and skiing. Bittermann & Sons paid the doctor's bill and Egger got two dazzling white plaster casts around his legs. At the end of the second week they stuffed a thick straw pillow behind his back and he was allowed to sit up and drink his milk from a mug instead of slurping it from an earthenware dish. At the end of the third week he was sufficiently recovered that every day, around noon, the innkeeper and the barman would wrap him in a horse blanket, lift him out of bed, and set him down outside the door on a little birchwood bench. From here he could see the slope where his house had stood, and where now all he could make out was a pile of debris illuminated by the warm spring sun.

Towards the end of May Egger asked one of the kitchen boys for a sharpened meat cleaver. He used it to cut and hack away at the plaster casts until he was able to break them into two halves, and his legs emerged. They lay there on the sheet, thin and white like two debarked sticks, looking to him almost more peculiar than a few weeks earlier when he had pulled them, stiff and cold, from the snow.

For a few days Egger dragged his emaciated body back and forth between the bed and the birchwood bench, until at last he felt that his legs belonged to him again and would be strong enough to carry him further. He slipped on a pair of trousers for the first time in weeks and headed off to his plot of land. He walked through the forest where it had been flattened by the avalanche; he looked up at the sky, which was full of small, round clouds, and at the flowers springing up everywhere between the stumps and the uprooted tree trunks: white, egg-yolk yellow, bright blue. He tried to see everything precisely so as to memorize it for later. He wanted to understand what had happened, but when, after several hours, he reached his plot and saw the beams and planks scattered about he knew there was nothing to understand. He sat on a rock and thought of Marie. He imagined what had happened that night, and saw terrible pictures in his mind's eye: Marie sitting upright in their bed, arms outstretched on the blanket, listening, wide-eyed, into the darkness a second before the avalanche smashed through the walls like a giant fist and drove her body into the cold earth.

* * *

In the autumn, almost half a year after the avalanche, Egger left the valley, moving on to work elsewhere for the company. But he couldn't do the heavy woodcutting any more.

'What are we supposed to do with someone like you?' asked the general manager. Egger had limped in sound-lessly across the carpet and was now standing in front of the desk, hanging his head. 'You're no good for anything any more.' Egger nodded, and the general manager sighed. 'I'm sorry about your wife,' he said. 'But don't go getting the idea that the blasting had anything to do with it. The last blast was a couple of weeks before the avalanche.'

'I'm not,' said Egger.

The general manager put his head on one side and stared out of the window for a while. 'Or do you think perhaps the mountain has a memory?' he asked abruptly. Egger shrugged. The manager leaned over, made a gargling noise and spat into a tin dish at his feet. 'All right,' he said at last. 'Bittermann & Sons has constructed seventeen cable cars so far, and believe you me, they won't be the last. People are all going crazy about slithering down mountains on their planks.' He pushed his dish under the desk with the tip of his shoe and looked at Egger solemnly. 'God alone knows why,' he said. 'At any rate, the cable cars have to be maintained: cables checked, impeller wheels lubricated, cabin roofs seen to and so on. You don't need solid ground under your feet all the time, do you?'

'Don't think so,' said Egger.

'That's all right, then,' said the general manager.

———

Egger was assigned to a small team, a handful of taciturn men whose bearded faces, burned by the mountain sun, betrayed almost nothing of their emotions. They travelled along mountain roads – more and more of which were tarmacked – perched on pallets in the back of a delivery truck, going from one cable car to another to take care of maintenance work that was too demanding for local workers. Egger's task was to sit in a wooden frame attached to the steel cables by nothing but a safety lanyard and a hand-braking roller mechanism, and to slide slowly down towards the valley, removing dust, ice and encrusted bird droppings from the cables and ball joints and lubricating them with fresh oil. No one else was keen to do this job. Word had got around that in previous years two men, both experienced climbers, had fallen to their deaths, through carelessness, or because of a material defect, or simply because of the wind, which sometimes made the cables swing out several metres on either side. But Egger wasn't afraid. He knew that his life hung from a thin rope, but as soon as he had scaled a girder, attached the roller mechanism and fastened the safety carabiner, a sense of calm came over him, and little by little the black cloud of confused, despairing thoughts that shrouded his heart dissolved in the mountain air, until nothing was left but pure sorrow.

For many months Egger moved on like this from valley to valley, sleeping in the truck or in cheap boarding-house rooms at night and dangling between heaven and earth by day. He saw winter settle over the mountains. He worked in thickly falling snow, scratched ice from the cables with his wire brush, and from the struts of girders he knocked long icicles that shattered quietly in the depths below him, or were noiselessly swallowed by the snow. Often, in the distance, he would hear the muffled rumble of an avalanche. Sometimes it would seem to come closer and he would look up the slope, anticipating an enormous white wave that would sweep him up for an instant and then overwhelm him, along with the cable, the steel girders and the whole world. But each time the rumbling died away and the clear cries of the jackdaws could be heard again.

In spring their route took him back to the valley, where he stayed for a while to clear brush and debris from Blue Liesl's forest aisle and fix small cracks in the girder foundations. He found lodgings at the Golden Goat again, in the room where he had spent so many days with his broken legs. Every evening he came back from the mountain dead tired, ate the remains of his daily ration sitting on the edge of his bed, and fell into a heavy, dreamless sleep as soon as his head hit the pillow. Once he awoke in the middle of the night with a peculiar sensation, and looking up at the small, dusty window under the ceiling he saw that it was clouded by hundreds of moths. The creatures' wings seemed to glow in the moonlight, and they beat against the pane with a barely discernible papery sound. For a moment Egger thought their appearance must be a sign, but he didn't know what it was supposed to mean, so he closed his eyes and tried to go back to sleep. They're only moths, he thought, a few silly little moths; and when he awoke early the next morning they had vanished.

He stayed several weeks in the village, which as far as he could tell had largely recovered from the impact of the avalanche, and then moved on. He avoided going to look at his plot of land or visiting the cemetery, and he didn't sit on the little birchwood bench. He moved on, hung in the air between mountains, and watched the seasons change beneath him like colourful paintings that meant nothing to him and had nothing to do with him. Later on he recalled the years after the avalanche as an empty, silent time that only slowly, almost imperceptibly, began to fill with life again.

One clear autumn day, when a roll of sandpaper slipped out of his hand and sprang down the slope like an impetuous young goat before eventually sailing out over a spur of rock and vanishing in the depths, Egger paused for the first time in years and contemplated his surroundings. The sun was low, and even the distant mountaintops stood out so clearly that it was as if someone had just finished painting them onto the sky. Right beside him a lone sycamore burned yellow; a little further off some cows were grazing, casting long, slim shadows that kept pace with them step for step across the meadow. A group of hikers was sitting beneath the canopy of a small calving shed. Egger could hear them talking and laughing amongst themselves, and their voices seemed to him both strange and agreeable. He thought of Marie's voice and how much he had liked to listen to it. He tried to recall its melody and sound, but they eluded him. 'If only I still had her voice, at least,' he said aloud to himself. Then he rolled slowly over to the next steel girder, climbed down and went in search of the sandpaper.

Three evenings later, after a cold, wet day spent scrubbing rust off the base rivets on a top station, Egger jumped down off the back of the truck and entered the little boarding house where he and the other men were staying. The way to his quarters took him past the landlady's living room with its smell of pickled gherkins. The old woman was sitting alone at the table. She had propped up her elbows and buried her face in her hands. In front of her was the big wireless set, which at this hour was usually blasting out brass-band music or Adolf Hitler's furious tirades. This time the radio was silent, and Egger could hear the old woman breathing quietly and heavily into her hands. 'Are you unwell?' he asked.

The landlady raised her head and looked at him. Her face retained the imprints of her fingers, pale stripes to which the blood only slowly returned. 'We're at war,' she said.

'Who says so?' asked Egger.

'The radio,' said the old woman, throwing a hostile look at the wireless. Egger watched as she reached behind her head and in two swift movements loosened her bun. The woman's hair fell onto her neck, long and yellowish, like flax fibres. For a moment her shoulders shook as if she was about to start sobbing; then she stood up, walked past him down the corridor and out into the open, where she was greeted by a grubby cat that wound itself about her feet for a while before the two of them disappeared around the corner.

The next morning Egger set off home to register for military service. His decision wasn't prompted by any particular considerations: it was simply there, all of a sudden, like a call from very far away, and Egger knew he had to follow it. He had been called up once before, when he was seventeen, for the army medical examination, but back then Kranzstocker had successfully lodged an objection, arguing that if they were to tear his beloved foster-son (who was also, incidentally, the most capable worker in the family) from his arms to use him as cannon-fodder against the wops or (worse still) the baguette-scoffers, they might as well in God's name just burn his whole farm down right under his arse. Back then, Egger was secretly grateful to the farmer: he'd had nothing in his life to lose, but at least he'd still had something to gain. That was different now.

As the weather was reasonably calm, he set off on foot. He walked all day, spent the night in an old hay barn and was up again before dawn. He listened to the steady hum of the telephone wires, recently strung along the roads between narrow poles, and he saw the mountains grow out of the night with the first rays of the sun, and although it was a spectacle he had watched thousands of times before, this time he found himself strangely moved by it. He couldn't remember ever in his life seeing something at once so beautiful and so terrifying.

Egger's stay in the village was brief. 'You're too old. And you limp,' said the officer who, along with the mayor and an elderly female typist, formed the examination committee. He was sitting in the Golden Goat, at one of the guesthouse tables, which was covered in a white tablecloth and decorated with little swastika flags.

'I want to go to war,' said Egger.

'Do you think the Wehrmacht can use someone like you?' asked the officer. 'Who do you think we are?'

'Don't be stupid, Andreas, go back to your work,' said the mayor. And that was the end of the matter. The typist stamped the single sheet of paper that constituted his file, and Egger returned to the cable cars.

Just over three years later, in November 1942, Egger stood before the same committee, not as a volunteer this time but as a conscript. He had no idea why the Wehrmacht suddenly could use someone like him after all: at any rate, it seemed that times had changed.

'What can you do?' the officer asked.

'I know about mountains,' answered Egger. 'I can sand steel cables and make holes in rock.'

'That's good,' the officer remarked. 'Have you ever heard of the Caucasus?'

'No,' said Egger.

'Never mind,' said the officer. 'Andreas Egger, I hereby declare you fit to go to war. You have been assigned the honourable task of liberating the East!'

Egger looked out of the window. It had started to rain: fat drops smacked against the window, darkening the restaurant. Out of the corner of his eye he saw the mayor slowly hunch over the table and stare down at its surface.

Egger spent a total of more than eight years in Russia. Less than two months of this were at the front; the rest was in a prisoner-of-war camp somewhere in the vast steppe north of the Black Sea. Although in the beginning his mission still seemed fairly clear (as well as liberating the East it was also about securing oil reserves and defending and maintaining planned production facilities), after just a few days he could no longer have said exactly why he was there, or for what or against whom he was actually fighting. It was as if in these pitch-dark Caucasian winter nights, when shell-fire blossomed like blazing flowers over the mountain crests on the horizon, casting its light on the soldiers' fearful or despairing or blank faces, any thought about purpose or the lack of it was stifled before it could be formulated. Egger questioned nothing. He carried out orders, that was all. Besides, he was of the opinion that he could have had it an awful lot worse. Just a few weeks after his arrival in the mountains, two taciturn comrades who were clearly familiar with the area brought him by night to a narrow rocky plateau at an altitude of around four thousand metres. One of his superiors had explained to him that he was to stay there until he was recalled, firstly to set a series of blast holes, secondly to secure the forward position and, if necessary, to hold it. Egger had no idea what forward position they were referring to or even what such a position might be, but he wasn't dissatisfied with his task. His two comrades left him there alone, with tools, a tent, a crate of provisions and the promise to return once a week with fresh supplies, and Egger made himself at home as best he could. During the day he bored dozens of holes in the rock, for which he often had first to hack away a thick layer of ice, and at night he lay in his tent and tried to sleep despite the biting cold. His equipment included a sleeping bag, two blankets, his fur-lined winter boots, and the thick, quilted jacket worn by mountain troops. He had also pitched the tent half inside a frozen snowdrift, and this provided him with at least a little shelter from the wind, which often howled so loudly that it drowned out the roaring of the bombers and the muffled explosions of the anti-aircraft guns. Yet all this was not enough to keep out the cold. The frost seemed to creep in through every seam, under clothing and under the skin, digging its claws into every fibre of his body. Making a fire was forbidden and punishable by death, but even had it been permitted, the plateau lay far above the tree line and for miles around there wasn't so much as a twig that Egger could have burned. Sometimes he would light the little petrol stove he used to heat the tinned food, but the tiny flames just seemed to mock him. They burned his fingertips and left the rest of his body to freeze all the more. Egger feared the nights. He lay huddled in his sleeping bag and the cold brought tears to his eyes. Sometimes he dreamed: confused dreams, filled with pain and hideous faces that materialized in the blizzard of his mind and hunted him down. Once he awoke from just such a dream because he thought that something soft and mobile had crept into the tent and was staring at him. 'Jesus!' he gasped softly. He waited until his heart had calmed again, then slipped from his sleeping bag and crawled out of the tent. The sky was starless and profoundly black. Everything around him was wrapped in darkness and altogether silent. Egger sat on a stone and stared out into the night. Again he heard his heart pounding, and at that moment he knew he was not alone. He couldn't say where this feeling came from; he saw only the blackness of the night and heard his heartbeat, but somewhere out there he sensed the presence of another living creature. He had no idea how long he sat like that in front of his tent, listening out into the darkness, but before the first pale strip of light appeared over the mountains he knew where this other creature was located. About thirty metres away, on the other side of the ravine that marked the western edge of the plateau, there was a spur that jutted out of the face of the rock, scarcely wide enough for a goat to gain a foothold. On the ledge stood a Russian soldier, his shape rapidly becoming clearer in the growing light of dawn. He was just standing there, inexplicably motionless, looking across at Egger, who for his part remained sitting on his stone, not daring to move. The soldier was young and had the milky face of a city boy. His forehead was smooth and snowy white, his eyes oddly slanting. He carried his weapon, a Cossack rifle without a bayonet, on a strap over his shoulder; his right hand lay calmly on the stock. The Russian looked at Egger and Egger looked at the Russian and around them was nothing but the silence of a Caucasian winter morning. Later, Egger could not have said which of them was first to move: a spasm passed through the soldier's body and, at the same time, Egger stood. The Russian removed his hand from the rifle stock and wiped his forehead with his sleeve. Then he turned and quickly, nimbly, without looking back, climbed up a few metres and disappeared between the rocks.

Egger stayed where he was for a moment, thinking. He realized that he had been standing face to face with his mortal enemy, yet now that the soldier had disappeared he felt his loneliness more profoundly than ever before.

At first his two comrades came every few days, as agreed, to stock up his food supplies and, when necessary, to bring a pair of woollen socks or a new rock drill, as well as news from the front (things were seesawing back and forth, there had been losses but also some gains, all in all no one really knew what was going on). But after a few weeks the visits stopped, and towards the end of December – Egger was scoring the days onto a sheet of ice with the drill, and by his count it must have been the day after Christmas – he started to suspect that they wouldn't be coming again. On the first of January 1943, after another week had gone by and still no one had turned up, he set off in thick, driving snow to walk back down to the camp. He followed the path they had come up almost two months earlier and was relieved when he soon saw the familiar red of the swastikas glimmering towards him. Within seconds, though, it abruptly dawned on him that the flags driven into the ground ahead to mark the camp perimeter were not swastikas at all, but the banners of the Russian Soviet Socialist Republic. In that moment Egger owed his life entirely to the presence of mind with which he immediately tore his rifle off his back and flung it as far away from him as he could. He saw the gun disappear into the snow with a muffled thud, and a split second later he heard the shouts of the guards running towards him. He raised his hands, fell to his knees and bowed his head. He felt a blow to the back of his neck, toppled forwards, and heard deep Russian voices speaking over him like incomprehensible sounds from another world.

For two days Egger crouched alongside two other prisoners in a wooden crate carelessly nailed together and sealed with felt. It had a length and breadth of about one and a half metres and was less than a metre high. He spent most of the time peering out through a slit, trying to glean from the movements around them some hint as to the Russians' plans, and his own future. When at last, on the third day, the nails were ripped from the wood with a screech and one of the slatted walls fell outwards, the winter light pierced his eyes so brightly that he feared he would never be able to open them again. He could, after a while; but this sensation of piercing brightness, which seemed to fill even his nights with blinding light, stayed with him until long after the end of his wartime captivity, and only disappeared for good many years after his return home.

The transfer to a camp near Voroshilovgrad took six days, which Egger spent in the midst of a group of prisoners herded together onto the back of an open truck. It was a terrible journey. They travelled through cold days and icy nights, beneath a dark sky shredded with shell-fire and across white, open snowfields where the stiff, frozen limbs of people and horses jutted from the furrows. Egger sat on the back of the truck and saw innumerable wooden crosses lining the road. He thought of the magazine Marie had read aloud to him so often, and of how little the winter landscape it depicted resembled this ice-bound, wounded world.

One of the prisoners, a small, stocky man trying to shield his head from the cold with the tattered shreds of a horse blanket, said the crosses were really not as sad as they appeared; they were just signposts indicating the direct route to Heaven. The man's name was Helmut Moidaschl and he laughed easily. He laughed about the snow that lashed their faces, and he laughed about the bricklike crusts of bread that were dumped out of a sack onto the back of the truck for them to eat. You'd be better off using that bread to build good, solid houses, he said, and laughed so loudly that their two Russian guards laughed with him. Sometimes he would wave to the old women examining the snow-covered corpses for useful items of clothing or food. If you're on the way to Hell, he'd say, you have to laugh with the devils: it costs nothing, and makes the whole thing more bearable.

Helmut Moidaschl was the first in a long line of people Egger saw die in Voroshilovgrad. The very night they arrived he was seized with a heavy fever, and his screams, stifled by the shreds of his blanket, filled the barracks for hours. The next morning they found him lying dead in a corner, half-naked, doubled over, both fists pressed against his temples.

After a few weeks Egger stopped counting the dead. They were buried in a little birch wood behind the camp. Death belonged to life like mould to bread. Death was a fever. It was hunger. It was a crack in the wall of the barracks and the winter wind whistling through.

Egger was assigned to a team of about a hundred workers. They worked in the forest or on the steppe, cut wood, built low walls with stones from the fields, helped out with the potato harvest or buried the previous night's dead. In winter he slept in the barracks with about two hundred other men. As soon as temperatures permitted he bedded down outdoors on a pile of straw. Ever since the warm night when someone had turned on the electric light by mistake and thousands of bugs had responded by trickling down from the ceiling, he preferred to sleep in the open air.

News of the end of the war reached Egger in one of the communal toilets. He was sitting on a plank above the cesspit with a swarm of glittering, greenish flies buzzing around him when the door was suddenly wrenched open and a Russian stuck in his head and bellowed, 'Hitler kaput! Hitler kaput!' Egger continued to sit there quietly and didn't respond, so the Russian slammed the door shut and walked away, laughing. His fading laughter could be heard outside for some time, until it was drowned by the wail of the mustering siren.

Less than three weeks later Egger had forgotten the guard's euphoria and the hopes it had awakened in him. The war was undeniably over, but this fact had no discernible repercussions on life in the camp. The work remained the same, the millet soup was thinner than ever, and the flies still circled unperturbed around the beams of the latrine. Besides, many of the prisoners believed that the end of the war could only be temporary. Maybe Hitler really was kaput, they argued, but behind every crackpot another, far worse crackpot was waiting in the wings, and ultimately it was only a matter of time before the whole thing started all over again.

On an unusually mild winter night Egger sat in front

of the barracks wrapped in his blanket and wrote a letter to his dead wife Marie. He had found an almost undamaged piece of paper and a pencil stub during a clean-up operation in a burnt-out village, and slowly, in big, wobbly letters, he wrote:

My dear Marie,

I am writing to you from Russia. It is not that bad here. There is work and something to eat, and because there are no mountains the sky is wider than the eye can see. The only really bad thing is the cold. It's a different cold to back home. If only I had just one little paraffin sack, like the ones I had so many of back then, it would be all right.

But I don't mean to complain. There are people lying stiff and cold in the snow and I am still looking at the stars. Perhaps you can see the stars, too. I'm afraid I have to end here. I only write slowly and it's already getting light behind the hills.

Your Egger

He folded the letter up as small as he could and buried it in the earth at his feet. Then he took his blanket and went back inside the barracks.

It was almost another six years before Egger's time in Russia came to an end. There was no prior warning of the liberation, but early one morning in the summer of 1951 the prisoners were herded together in the square in front of the barracks, where they were made to strip naked and throw their clothes on top of one another in a great, stinking heap. The heap was doused in petrol and set alight, and as the men stared into the flames the fear that they were about to be shot, or worse, was written on their faces. But the Russians were laughing and all talking loudly at once, and when one of them grabbed a prisoner by the shoulder, pulled him close and proceeded to lead the naked, scrawny spectre in a ridiculous dance around the fire, it began to dawn on most of them that this morning was a good morning.

Furnished with fresh items of clothing and a crust of bread apiece, the men left the camp within the hour to set off on the march to the nearest train station. Egger had slipped into one of the rows at the back. Directly in front of him walked a young man with big, permanently frightened eyes who started gobbling his bread in greedy bites as soon as they set off. When he had swallowed the last scrap he turned again and glanced back at the camp, which already lay some kilometres behind them and was scarcely visible now in the shimmering summer air. He grinned and opened his mouth to say something, but all that came out was a choking sound, and then he began to cry. He howled and sobbed and the tears and snot flowed down his dirty cheeks in wide streaks. One of the older men, tall with a shock of white hair and a disgruntled expression, walked up to the boy, put an arm round his shaking shoulders and told him to stop crying, firstly because all it did was give you a soggy collar, and secondly because bawling was as infectious as horse-fever and bubonic plague put together and he had no desire to spend the two-thousand-kilometre journey home surrounded by grizzling old women. On top of which he'd be better off saving his tears for when he got back, because there'd be plenty more for him to cry about there. The young man stopped weeping and for a long time Egger, walking two steps behind him, could hear the dry sounds he made as he swallowed his tears and the very last crumbs of bread.

* * *

After his return home Egger initially lived behind the newly erected school building, in a wooden shack that the local authority, with the mayor's benevolent support, made over to him. The mayor was no longer a Nazi these days; geraniums hung outside the windows again instead of swastikas, and in other respects, too, much in the village had changed. The road had got wider. Motor vehicles rattled past many times a day, often at quite short intervals, and the stinking, smoking trucks, those old diesel monstrosities, were increasingly seldom among them. Shining automobiles of every colour came hurtling in from the top of the valley, spitting out day-trippers, hikers and skiers onto the village square. Many of the farmers rented out guestrooms, and the chickens and pigs had disappeared from most of the sheds. Skis and hiking poles now stood in their place, and the pens smelled of wax instead of chicken and pig shit. The Golden Goat had acquired competition. Every day the landlord of the Goat would work himself into a lather again about the Mitterhofer guesthouse that had recently been built across the way, with its resplendent lime-green facade and the sign above the door offering shiny words of welcome. He hated old Mitterhofer. He refused to understand how a cattle farmer could suddenly hit on the idea of setting aside his pitchfork and providing accommodation for tourists instead of cows. 'A farmer is a farmer and will never be an inn-keeper!' he said. Secretly, though, he had to admit that the competition wasn't bad for business: on the contrary, it invigorated it. When he eventually died in the late Sixties, a scatterbrained old man, he was able to bequeath to his only daughter, in addition to the Golden Goat, another three guesthouses, several hectares of land, the bowling alley under the stables of the former Loidolt farm, and shares in two chair lifts, which, although she was well on the wrong side of forty, turned this unmarried and rather obdurate woman into one of the most desirable catches in the valley.

Egger accepted all these changes with silent amaze-ment. At night he would hear in the distance the metallic creak of the marker poles on the slopes – or pistes, as they were now called – and in the morning he was often woken by the clamour of the schoolchildren behind the wall at the head of his bed. This would break off abruptly the moment the teacher entered the classroom. He remem-bered his own childhood, his few years of school, which at the time had stretched out endlessly before him and now seemed as brief and fleeting as the blink of an eye. All in all, time bewildered him. The past seemed to curve in all directions, and in memory the sequence of events became confused, or would constantly reform and re-evaluate itself in peculiar ways. He had spent far more time in Russia than he had with Marie, yet the years in the Caucasus and Voroshilovgrad seemed scarcely longer than his last few days with her. His time with the cable cars shrank in retrospect to a single season, whereas he felt as if he had spent half his life hanging over an ox yoke looking at the ground, his little white bottom stretched towards the evening sky.

A few weeks after his return, Egger came across old Kranzstocker. He was sitting in front of his farm on a rickety milking stool, and Egger greeted him as he walked past. Kranzstocker slowly lifted his head: it was a while before he recognized Egger. 'You,' he said, in an ancient, croaking voice. 'You, of all people!' Egger stopped and looked at the old man, sitting there, slumped, peering up at him from yellow eyes. The hands on his knees were thin as kindling; his mouth hung half open and seemed to be entirely devoid of teeth. Egger had heard that two of his sons had not returned from the war, whereupon he had tried to hang himself from the pantry doorframe. The brittle wood had not withstood his weight and Kranz-stocker had survived. From then on the old farmer had spent his days yearning for death. He saw Death crouched on every corner, and each evening he was convinced that eternal rest would descend on him with the darkness. But he always woke again the next day, even sicker, more morose, more corroded by his yearning than before.

'Come over here,' he said, craning his head forwards like a chicken. 'Let's see what you look like!' Egger took a step towards him. The old man's cheeks were sunken, and his hair, once gleaming black, now hung from his skull as white and thin as cobwebs. 'It'll soon be over for me, Death misses no one,' he said. 'Every day I hear him coming round the corner, but every time it's just one of the neighbour's cows or a dog or the shadow of some other creeping creature.' Egger stood as if rooted to the spot. For a moment he felt as if he were a child again, and he was afraid the old man might get to his feet and rise up tall as a mountain. 'And so today it's you,' the farmer continued. 'Someone like you just comes round the corner, and others don't come anywhere any more. That's justice for you. I was Kranzstocker once, and now look at me, what's become of me: a heap of rotting bones with just enough life left in them not to crumble to dust on the spot. All my life I walked upright, I bowed to the Lord and no one else. And how does the Lord thank me? By taking two of my sons. By tearing my own flesh and blood from my body. And because that still isn't enough for him, the son of a bitch, because he still hasn't squeezed the last drop of life out of an old farmer like me, he lets me sit outside my farm every day from morning till night waiting for Death. So here I sit, wearing my backside to the bone, but the only things that come round the corner are a couple of cows and a couple of shadows and you – you, of all people!'

Kranzstocker looked down at his hands, at his thin, mottled fingers. His breath came heavily, with a quiet rattle. Suddenly he raised his head, and at the same time one of the hands shot out of his lap and grabbed Egger's forearm.

'You can do it now!' he cried, his voice trembling with agitation. 'You can strike me now! Strike me, you hear? I'm begging you, strike me! Please, just strike me dead!' Egger felt the old man's fingers digging into his arm, and an icy fear gripped his heart. He pulled away and took a step back. Kranzstocker dropped his hand and sat there silently, his eyes again fixed on the ground. Egger turned and left.

As he walked along the road that ended just behind the village, he had a strange empty feeling in his stomach. Deep down, he felt sorry for the old farmer. He thought of the milking stool and wished he could have a chair and a warm blanket, and at the same time he wished he could have death. He went on along the narrow path up the mountain, all the way to the Pichlersenke. Up here the ground was soft and the grass short and dark. Drops of water trembled on the tips of the blades, making the whole meadow glitter as if studded with glass beads. Egger marvelled at these tiny, trembling drops that clung so tenaciously to the blades of grass, only to fall at last and seep into the earth or dissolve to nothing in the air.

It was only many years later that Kranzstocker found release, on an autumn day in the late Seventies, as he sat like a shadow listening to the radio in his room. In order to understand anything at all he had leaned his body right over the table and was pressing his left ear against the speaker. When the presenter announced that the next programme would be a concert of brass-band music the old man gave a sudden cry, pounded his fist repeatedly against his ribs, and finally slid off the chair, stiff and dead, to the music's tinny, rhythmical accompaniment.

During the funeral it bucketed down. The road was flooded with ankle-deep mud and the funeral procession could make only slow progress. Egger, himself by this time over seventy, walked right at the back. He thought about the farmer, who had spent all his life thrashing his own happiness away from him. They were walking in the pouring rain past the little restaurant in what used to be the Achmandl farm when a child's laughter rang out, loudly and with remarkable clarity. One of the windows was ajar and flickering brightly. The landlord's little son was sitting in the room in front of an enormous television set, his face right up against the screen. The reflection of the images danced across his forehead; he was clutching the antenna with one hand and slapping his thighs with the other as he laughed. He was laughing so hard that through the curtain of rain Egger could make out the glistening drops of spittle spraying against the box. He felt an urge to stop and stand there, to press his forehead against the window and laugh along with the boy. But the funeral procession moved on, dark and silent. Egger saw before him the hunched shoulders of the mourners and the rain running down them in thin rivulets. At the head of the procession the coffin cart rocked like a boat in the gathering dusk as the child's laughter gradually faded away behind them.

Although in the course of his life Egger did give the idea some consideration, he never got himself a television set. Usually he had no money or no space or no time, and in any case it seemed to him that, generally speaking, he lacked all the necessary prerequisites for such an invest-ment. For instance, he could barely muster the stamina with which most other people would stare for hours into the flickering screen, something he secretly assumed could, in the long run, damage your eyesight and soften your brain. Yet television gave him two moments that made a very deep impression on him, and which in later years he would repeatedly drag up from the depths of his memory, recalling them with a little shock of pleasure. The first was one evening in the back room of the Golden Goat, where a brand-new Imperial television set had stood for some time. Egger hadn't been to the inn for months, and was therefore surprised when, on entering, he was assailed by tinny television voices over a quiet hiss of static, rather than by the customary public-house murmur. He went to the back, where seven or eight people sat scattered at different tables, staring mesmerized into an appliance the size of a wardrobe. For the first time in his life Egger saw the television images close to. They moved before his eyes with magical ease, bringing to the stuffy back room of the Golden Goat a world about which, until now, he had not had the slightest notion. He saw narrow, soaring houses with roofs that stuck up into the sky like inverted icicles. Scraps of paper were snowing from the windows and the people on the street were laughing, shouting, flinging their hats into the air, and generally seemed to be quite mad with joy. Before Egger could take it all in the screen was torn apart, as if by a soundless explosion, only to recombine less than a second later in an entirely different scene. Men in short-sleeved shirts and workers' overalls were sitting on some wooden benches watching a dark-skinned girl of about ten, who was kneeling in a cage stroking the mane of a lion that lay sprawled before her. The animal yawned and you could see right into its mouth, which was criss-crossed with thin threads of saliva. The audience applauded, the girl snuggled up to the lion's body and for a moment it looked as if she was about to disappear into its mane. Egger laughed. He did so more out of embarrassment, as he had no idea how one was supposed to behave in front of the television in the presence of others. He was ashamed of his ignorance. He felt like a child observing the incomprehensible activities of adults: it was all somehow interesting, but none of it seemed to have anything to do with him personally.

And then he saw something that touched the very depths of his heart. A young woman was emerging from an aeroplane. It wasn't just any woman who was walking down the narrow staircase to the runway; it was the most beautiful creature Egger had seen in his life. She was called Grace Kelly, a name that to his ears sounded strange and outrageous, but at the same time it seemed to be the only name that was fitting. She was wearing a short coat and waving to a huddled crowd of people who had gathered at the airfield. A handful of reporters dashed up, and as she answered their breathless questions the sunlight flowed over her blonde hair and across her smooth, slender neck. Egger shivered at the thought that this hair and this neck were not just an illusion, but that somewhere in this world there might be someone who had touched them with their fingers, perhaps even stroked them with the whole of their hand. Grace Kelly waved again, laughing with a dark, wide-open mouth. Egger got up and left the inn. For a while he walked aimlessly about the village streets before finally sitting down on the steps at the entrance to the chapel. He stared at the ground, trodden flat by countless generations of sinners, and waited for his heart to stop pounding. Grace Kelly's smile and the sadness in her eyes had churned up his emotions and he didn't understand what he was feeling. He sat there for a long while until, some time after darkness had fallen, he realized how cold it was, and went home.

That was in the late Fifties. It was only much later, in the summer of 1969, that Egger had a second encounter with the television – which in most households by then already constituted the central focus and primary purpose of the evening family gathering – that made a profound impression on him, albeit in an entirely different way. This time he was sitting with almost a hundred and fifty other villagers in the assembly room of the new parish hall, watching two young Americans walk on the Moon for the first time. There was a tense silence in the room for almost the whole of the broadcast, yet scarcely had Neil Armstrong set foot on the Moon's dusty surface than everyone started cheering, and for a few moments at least it was as if some kind of burden fell from the farmers' heavy shoulders. Afterwards there was free beer for the adults and juice and doughnuts for the children, and a member of the parish council gave a short speech about the tremendous endeavours that made such marvels possible and would probably drive humanity on goodness knows whither. Egger applauded with everyone else. As the ghostly apparitions continued to move within the television set before them – the Americans who, incomprehensibly, were at that moment high above their heads, strolling across the surface of the Moon – he felt mysteriously close and connected to the villagers down here on the darkened Earth, in a room in the parish hall that still smelled of fresh mortar.

The very day he got back from Russia, Egger had headed straight to the camp of the firm Bittermann & Sons. If he had asked someone beforehand he could have saved himself the walk. The barracks were gone. The camp had been dismantled. Here and there a patch of concrete or a wooden beam overgrown with weeds still indicated that people had once worked and lived here. Little white flowers now blossomed on the spot where the general manager had sat behind his desk.

In the village Egger discovered that the company had gone bankrupt just after the war. The last remaining workers were pulled out a year earlier, as the firm responded to the Fatherland's by then desperate call and switched production from steel girders and double cable winches to weaponry. Old Bittermann, a fervent patriot who in the First World War had left one forearm and a splinter of his right cheekbone in a trench on the Western front, concentrated on the manufacture of carbine barrels and ball-and-socket joints for assault guns. The joints were sound, but part of the magazine warped in extreme heat, which resulted in a number of dreadful accidents at the front and finally led old Bittermann to believe he was in no small measure complicit in the loss of the war. He shot himself in a copse behind his house – with his father's old hunting rifle, to be on the safe side. When the forest ranger found his body under a stunted crab apple, a metal plate engraved with the date *23.11.1917* glinted out at him from inside the shattered skull.

The cable cars were now built and run by other enterprises, but wherever Egger presented himself they sent him away again. He wasn't quite right any more, they said. The few years since the war had been enough for many of the old procedures to be updated, which was why, regrettably, in the world of modern transport engineering there was no longer any place for a man like him.

At home in the evenings Egger sat on the edge of his bed and regarded his hands. They lay in his lap, heavy and dark as bog soil. The skin was leathery and furrowed like the skin of an animal. The many years on the rock and in the forest had left scars, and each of those scars could have told a tale of mishap, effort, or success, if Egger had been able to remember their stories. Ever since the night when he had dug in the snow for Marie, his fingernails had been brittle and ingrown around the edges. One of his thumbnails was black, with a small dent in the middle. Egger brought his hands close to his face and contemplated the skin on the backs, which looked in places like crumpled linen. He saw the calluses on his fingertips and the gnarled bulges on his knuckles. Dirt which neither horse brush nor hard soap could dislodge had settled in the cracks and creases. Egger saw the pattern of the veins beneath the skin, and when he raised his hands against the half-light of the window he could see that they trembled very slightly. They were the hands of an old man, and he let them fall.

For a while Egger lived on the demobilization payments for war veterans. However, as the money was scarcely enough for the bare necessities, he found himself forced to take on all kinds of casual jobs, just as he had when he was a young man. Now as then he crawled around in cellars and in hay, hauled sacks of potatoes, toiled in the fields or mucked out the few remaining cowsheds and pigpens. He could still keep up with his younger colleagues, and some days he would get them to pile an impressive three-metre heap of hay onto his back with which he would trudge slowly downhill, swaying, over the steep pastures. But in the evening he would fall into bed convinced that he would never be able to get up again unaided. His crooked leg was now virtually numb around the knee, and whenever he turned his head so much as a centimetre to the side a stabbing pain in the back of his neck ran like a burning thread right down to his fingertips, forcing him to lie on his back and wait, motionless, for sleep.

One summer morning in the year 1957 Egger crawled out of bed long before sunrise and went outside. His pains had woken him, and the exercise in the cool night air did him good. He took the Geissensteig, the goat path, across the communal meadows that curved gently in the moonlight, and circled the two lumps of rock that reared up like the backs of sleeping animals. Finally, after hiking for almost an hour over increasingly difficult terrain, he reached the rock formations just below the Klufterspitze. By now day had announced itself, and in the distance the snow-capped peaks were starting to glow. Egger was about to sit down with his penknife to cut a torn piece of leather off his sole when an old man popped up from behind a rock and approached him with outstretched arms. 'My dear, dear sir!' he cried. 'You are a real human being, aren't you?'

'I believe so,' said Egger, and saw a second figure, an old woman, stumble out from behind the rock. They both looked pitiful, confused and trembling with exhaustion and cold.

The man was about to rush towards Egger when he saw the knife in his hand and stopped.

'You're not going to kill us, are you?' he said, aghast.

'God in Heaven, have mercy,' murmured the woman behind him.

Egger put the knife away without speaking and looked straight at the two old people, who stared at him, wide-eyed.

'My dear sir,' the man repeated; he seemed to be on the verge of tears. 'We have been walking around all night in this place where there is nothing but stones!'

'Nothing but stones!' the woman agreed.

'More stones than there are stars in the sky!'

'God in Heaven, have mercy.'

'We lost our way.'

'Wherever you look, nothing but cold, dark night!'

'And stones!' said the old man, who now actually did shed a couple of tears that ran down his cheek and neck one after the other. His wife looked at Egger imploringly.

'My husband was on the brink of lying down to die.'

'Our name is Roskovics,' the old man said, 'and we've been married for forty-eight years. That's almost half a century. You know then what you have in each other, and what you are to each other. Do you understand, sir?'

'Not really,' said Egger. 'And anyway, I'm not a sir. But I can take you down now, if you want.'

When they arrived in the village Mr Roskovics insisted on clasping the reluctant Egger to his bosom.

'Thank you!' he said, deeply moved.

'Yes, thank you!' echoed his wife.

'Thank you! Thank you!'

'Yes, all right,' said Egger, stepping back. On the way down from the Klufterspitze the couple's anxiety and despair had quickly dissipated, and when the first rays of sun warmed their faces their tiredness too suddenly seemed to disappear. Egger had shown them how to sip morning dew from the mountain grass to quench their thirst, and they had walked behind him chattering like children almost the whole way.

'We wanted to ask you,' said Roskovics, 'whether you might be able to show us a couple of trails. You seem to know the region like your own back garden.'

'For the likes of us, a hiking tour of this kind is not a walk in the park!' his wife agreed.

'Only a couple of days. Just up the mountain and down again. Money's no object; we wouldn't want to leave a bad impression. So – what do you reckon?'

Egger thought about the days ahead. There were a couple of metres of firewood to be chopped, and a potato field that had slipped in the rain and needed to be re-ploughed. The thought of the plough stilts in his hands filled him with dread. After just a few hours they began to burn red-hot beneath the fingers: even the hardest of calluses offered no protection against them.

'Yes,' he said. 'That might work out.'

For a whole week Egger led the two old people over increasingly challenging paths and showed them the beauties of the region. The work gave him pleasure. Hillwalking came easily to him, and the mountain air blew the gloomy thoughts from his head. There was also, in his view, an agreeable lack of conversation, partly because there wasn't much to talk about in any case, and partly because the couple behind him were too out of breath to wring unnecessary words from their quietly whistling lungs.

When the week was over the two of them bade him an effusive farewell, and Mr Roskovics stuck a couple of banknotes in Egger's jacket pocket. He and his wife were positively misty-eyed when they finally got into their car and headed home, disappearing along a road still thick with early morning fog.

Egger had enjoyed this new task. He painted a sign which he felt contained the most essential information and was also somehow interesting enough to entice tourists to engage his services, stationed himself with it directly beside the fountain in the village square, and waited.

IF YOU LIKE THE MOUNTAINS
I'M YOUR MAN.

I (with practically a lifetime's experience
in and of Nature) offer:

Hiking with or without baggage

Excursions (half or full day)

Climbing trips

Walks in the mountains (for senior citizens,

disabled people and children)

Guided tours in all seasons (weather permitting)

Guaranteed sunrise for early birds

Guaranteed sunset (in the valley only,
as too dangerous on the mountain)

No danger to life and limb!

(PRICE IS NEGOTIABLE,
BUT NOT EXPENSIVE)

The sign evidently made an impression because business was good from the start, such that Egger had no reason to go back to his old work as an odd-job man. As before, he often got up when it was still dark, but now instead of going out into the fields he went up into the mountains and watched the rising sun. In the reflection of its first rays the tourists' faces looked as if they were glowing from the inside, and Egger saw that they were happy.

In summer his tours often went well beyond the crests of the nearest mountains, while in winter he mostly confined himself to shorter walks, which in wide snowshoes were scarcely less exhausting. He always led the way, with an eye on potential dangers and the tourists panting at his back. He liked these people, even if some of them did try to explain the world to him or behaved idiotically in some other way. He knew that during a two-hour uphill climb, if not before, their arrogance would evaporate along with the sweat on their hot heads, until nothing remained but gratitude that they had made it and a tiredness deep in the bones.

Sometimes he would pass his old plot of land. Over the years scree had accumulated on the spot where once his house had stood, forming a sort of embankment.

In summer white poppies glowed between the lumps of stone, and in winter the children jumped over it on their skis. Egger would watch them whizzing down the slope, taking off with a whoop and sailing for a moment through the air before landing skilfully or tumbling through the snow like brightly coloured balls. He thought of the threshold where he and Marie had sat on so many evenings, and of the little wooden gate with the simple hook he had fashioned from a long steel nail. After the avalanche the gate had vanished, like so many other things that failed to reappear once the snow had melted. They were simply gone, as if they had never been. Egger felt the sadness well up in his heart. He thought that there would have been so much more for her to do with her life, probably far more than he could imagine.

Egger didn't usually speak on his walks. 'When someone opens their mouth they close their ears,' Thomas Mattl had always said, and Egger was of the same opinion. Instead of talking, he preferred to listen to these people, whose breathless chatter revealed to him the secrets of other fates and opinions. People were evidently looking for something in the mountains that they believed they had lost a long time ago. He never worked out what exactly this was, but over the years he became more and more certain that the tourists were stumbling not so much after him but after some obscure, insatiable longing.

Once, during a short break at the top of the Zwanzigerkogel, a young man grabbed him by the shoulders, quivering with emotion, and screamed at him, 'Can't you see how beautiful all this is!' Egger looked into the man's face, contorted with bliss, and said, 'Yes, but it's going to rain soon, and when the earth starts to slide you can forget about all the beauty.'

Only once in his career as a mountain guide did Egger almost lose a tourist. It was on a spring day sometime in the late Sixties; winter had returned again overnight, and Egger wanted to take a small group along the panoramic route above the new four-chair lift. As they were crossing the footbridge over the Häusler ravine, a fat lady slipped on the wet wood and lost her balance. Egger was walking right in front of her: out of the corner of his eye he saw her flailing her arms, and one of her legs rose up as if pulled into the air on an invisible string. Beneath the bridge was a twenty-metre drop. As he lunged towards her, his eyes were fixed on her face, tilting further and further back as if stricken with profound awe. He heard the wood groan as she crashed onto her back. At the very last moment, before she could slide over the edge and down into the abyss, he managed to seize one of her ankles with his hand, and even as he was marvelling at the unwontedly soft flesh beneath his fingers, his other hand grabbed her sleeve and he dragged her back onto the bridge, where she lay still, apparently contemplating the clouds with amazement.

'That almost ended badly, didn't it?' she said. She took Egger's hand, placed it on her cheek and smiled at him. Egger nodded, shocked. The skin of her cheek was damp. He sensed a barely perceptible quivering beneath his palm, and the contact seemed to him somehow improper. He was reminded of an experience from his childhood, when he was about eleven years old. The farmer had got him out of bed in the middle of the night: he had to help him deliver a calf. The cow had been labouring for hours, walking restlessly in circles and rubbing her muzzle on the wall until it bled. Finally she made a stifled noise and lay down on her side in the straw. In the flickering light of the kerosene lamp little Egger saw her roll her eyes and a glutinous slime flow from her cleft. When the calf's front legs appeared, the farmer, who had been sitting on his stool throughout in silence, stood and rolled up his sleeves. But the calf didn't move again, and the cow just lay there quietly. Suddenly she raised her head and began to bellow. It was a sound that filled Egger's heart with cold horror. 'It's done for!' said the farmer, and together they dragged the dead calf out of its mother's body. Egger caught hold of the neck. The hide was soft and wet, and for a brief moment he thought he felt a pulse, a solitary throb beneath his fingers. He held his breath, but nothing followed, and the farmer carried the limp body out into the open. Outside day was already breaking. Little Egger stood in the stall, cleaned the floor, rubbed down the cow's hide with straw and thought of the calf, whose life had lasted just a single heartbeat.

The fat lady smiled. 'I think everything's still in one piece,' she said. 'My thigh hurts a bit, but that's all. Now the two of us can limp down to the valley side by side.'

'No,' said Egger, and stood up. 'Every one of us limps alone!'

Since Marie's death Egger had, from time to time, carried clumsy female tourists over a mountain stream or led them by the hand over a slippery ridge of rock, but apart from that he had never touched a woman more than fleet-ingly. It had been hard enough somehow to adapt to life again, and under no circumstances did he wish to forfeit the calm that had grown in him over the years. When it came down to it he had barely even understood Marie, and all other women were far more of a mystery to him. He didn't know what they wanted or didn't want, and much of what they said and did in his presence confused him, infuriated him, or provoked in him a kind of inner rigidity which he found very hard to shake off. On one occasion one of the seasonal workers thrust her heavy body with its kitchen smell up against him in the Golden Goat and whispered clammy words in his ear, which so flustered him that he rushed out of the inn without paying for his soup and spent half the night trudging over the frozen slopes to calm down.

There were often moments like these that had the capacity to stir him, but they occurred less frequently with every passing year and eventually ceased altogether. He was not unhappy about this. He had had a love, and he had lost her. Nothing comparable would ever happen to him again: that, for Egger, was a given. The struggle with lust, which still surged up in him from time to time, was a struggle he intended to conduct with himself, on his own, until the end.

In the early Seventies, however, Andreas Egger had another encounter which, for a few brief autumn days at least, conflicted with his desire to spend the rest of his life alone. Recently he had noticed that the atmosphere in the classroom behind his bedroom wall had changed. The children's customary shouting had got louder, and when the break bell went, their outbursts and cheers of relief seemed to lack all inhibition. The reason for the pupils' newly acquired, raucous self-confidence was clearly the retirement of the village schoolmaster, a man who had spent most of his life trying to implant at least the basic principles of reading and arithmetic in the lazy-minded heads of generations of farmers' children, most of whom never thought beyond the here and now: if necessary, he would call on the assistance of a cudgel he had fashioned himself from an oxtail. After his final lesson the old teacher opened the window, tipped the box with the remaining pieces of chalk into the rose bed and turned his back on the village the very same day. This caused consternation among the local council members, particularly as they were unlikely to find a successor overnight who was keen to advance their career surrounded by herds of cows and skiers. A solution was found in the shape of Anna Holler, a teacher from the neighbouring valley who had retired many years ago, and who accepted the offer to fill in at the school with quiet gratitude. Anna Holler's ideas about education differed from those of her predecessor. She trusted in the children's innate powers of development, and she hung the old oxtail outside on the schoolhouse wall, where it weathered with the years and became a support for the wild ivy.

Egger, however, took a dim view of the new pedagogy. One morning he got up and went next door.

'Excuse me, but it's too loud. A man needs his peace and quiet, after all.'

'Who in heaven's name are you?'

'My name is Egger and I live next door. My bed must be about here, right behind the blackboard.'

The teacher took a step towards him. She was at least a head and a half smaller, but with the children behind her, staring at Egger from their rows of seats, she appeared threatening and entirely unprepared to compromise. He would have liked to say more; instead, he just gazed mutely down at the linoleum. Suddenly he felt stupid standing there: an old man with ridiculous complaints, someone even little children could stare at in undisguised astonishment.

'We can't choose our neighbours,' said the teacher, 'but one thing's for sure: you are an ill-mannered oaf! You burst into the middle of my lesson, uninvited, unshaven, hair uncombed, and to cap it all still in your underpants, or what's that supposed to be you've got on?'

'Leggings,' murmured Egger, who was already bitterly regretting having come round. 'They've been patched a few times.'

Anna Holler sighed. 'You will leave my classroom immediately,' she said. 'And when you have washed, shaved, and dressed properly you may come back again, if you wish!'

Egger didn't come back again. He would put up with the noise, or stuff moss in his ears if necessary: for him, the matter was settled. And that would probably have been the end of it, had there not been three loud knocks on his door the following Sunday. Anna Holler was standing outside with a cake in her hands.

'I thought I'd bring you something to eat,' she said. 'Where's the table?'

Egger offered her his only seat, a milking stool he had made himself, and placed the cake on his old storage chest in which, out of a secret fear of hard times, he kept a few cans of tinned food – 'Haggemeyer's Finest Beef with Onions' – and a pair of warm shoes. 'Cakes like this are often very dry,' he said, and as he set off with his earthenware jug to the fountain in the village square, he thought about this woman who was right now sitting in his room, waiting to cut the cake. He thought she might be about his age, but the many years of teaching had visibly taken their toll. Her face was wreathed in tiny wrinkles and under her dark hair, which she wore tied back in a tight bun, the snow-white roots shimmered through. For a moment a peculiar image thrust itself upon him: he saw her not simply sitting waiting on his stool, but had the impression that her mere presence had altered the room he had inhabited alone for so many years, had expanded it, had in some unpleasant way opened it up on all sides.

'So this is where you live,' said the teacher, when he returned with the jug full of water.

'Yes,' he said.

'One can be happy anywhere, really,' she said. She had dark brown eyes that were warm and friendly, yet Egger found it uncomfortable to be looked at by her. He glanced down at his piece of cake, pressed out a raisin with his forefinger and let it fall discreetly to the floor. Then they ate, and he had to admit that the cake was good. Actually, he thought, the cake was probably better than anything he had eaten in recent years; but this he kept to himself.

Later Egger could not have said how the whole affair came to pass. Just as Anna Holler had quite naturally appeared outside his door with the cake in her hands, she quite naturally walked into his life, where within a very short time she was claiming the space that she clearly assumed was hers. Egger didn't really know what was happening; besides which he didn't want to be rude, so he went for walks with her or sat beside her in the sun and drank the coffee she always brought along in a thermos, which she declared was blacker than the soul of Satan. Anna Holler was constantly coming out with comparisons like these; in fact, she talked virtually non-stop, telling him about her lessons, about the children, about her life, about this one man who had long since got what was coming to him and whom she should never, never, never have trusted. Sometimes she said something Egger didn't understand. She used words he had never heard before, and he secretly assumed she just made them up when she had run out of all the right ones. He let her talk. He listened, nodded from time to time, occasionally said yes or no, and drank the coffee, which made his heart race as if he were scaling the north face of the High Kämmerer.

One day she persuaded him to take Blue Liesl up to the Karleitner summit. From up there you could look out over the whole village, she said; the school looked like a lost matchbox, and if you squinted a bit you could just see the bright dots of the children around the village fountain.

When the gondola started with a slight jolt, Egger positioned himself at one of the windows. He felt the teacher come and stand right behind him and look over his shoulder. He thought of the fact that he hadn't washed his jacket in years. At least he had hung his trousers in the clear water of the spring for half an hour last week, drying them afterwards on a sunny rock.

'You see that girder down there?' he said. 'When we were pouring the foundation, someone fell in. Drank too much the day before and keeled over at midday. Face down in the concrete. Lay there and didn't move. Like a dead fish in a pond. It was a while before we managed to get him out; the concrete wasn't that liquid any more. But he made it. He's been blind in one eye ever since, though. Hard to say whether it was the concrete or the Krauterer.'

Once they reached the top they stood on the platform for a while looking down into the valley. Egger felt as if he ought to entertain the teacher, so he pointed out various things in the village: the remains of a burnt-out cattle shed, the complex of holiday homes hastily built on a beet field, the huge cauldron, overgrown with rust and purple broom, that the mountain infantry had left standing behind the chapel at the end of the war and which the children had used ever since for their games of hide and seek. Anna Holler laughed out loud every time she made out something new. Sometimes her laugh was completely swallowed by the wind, so that it looked as if she was just beaming away silently to herself.

When they got back to the valley station in the early evening they stood side by side for a little while and watched the cabin heading back up the mountain. Egger didn't know what he was supposed to say, or whether he was supposed to say anything at all, so he kept his mouth shut. The muffled whirring of the engines could be heard coming up from the machine room in the basement of the building. He felt the teacher's eyes upon him. 'I'd like you to take me home now,' she said, and walked off.

She was living in a little room right behind the town hall which the municipality had put at her disposal while she covered at the school. She had prepared a plate with a couple of slices of bread and dripping garnished with onion, and outside on the window ledge were two cold bottles of beer. Egger ate the bread and drank the beer, trying not to look at the teacher as he did so.

'You're a man,' she said. 'A real man with a real appetite, aren't you?'

'Maybe,' he said, and shrugged.

It was beginning to get dark outside. She stood up, took a few steps across the room, and stopped in front of a little dresser. From behind Egger saw her lower her head as if she had lost something on the floorboards. Her fingers were playing with the hem of her skirt. Earth and dust still stuck to her heels. It was dreadfully silent in the room. It was as if the silence that had withdrawn from all the valleys long ago was gathering right at this moment, right here in this little room. Egger cleared his throat. He put down his bottle and watched a drop run slowly down the glass and spread out on the tablecloth in a round, dark stain. Anna Holler stood in front of the dresser, motion-less, eyes lowered. She raised first her head, then her hands.

'People are often alone in this world,' she said.

Then she turned around. She lit two candles and placed them on the table. Closed the curtains. Pushed the bolt across the door.

'Come,' she said.

Egger was still staring at the dark stain on the table-cloth. 'I've only ever lain with one woman,' he said.

'That doesn't matter,' said the teacher. 'I'm fine with that.'

Later, Egger looked at the sleeping old woman who lay beside him. After they had gone to bed she had placed her hand on his chest, and beneath it his heart had pounded so loudly that he thought the whole room was moving. It hadn't worked out. He wasn't able to overcome his inhibitions. He had lain there motionless, as if nailed to the spot, feeling the hand grow heavier and heavier on his chest until finally it sank between his ribs and settled directly over his heart. He looked at her body. She was lying on her side. Her head had slipped off the pillow and her hair lay in thin strands on the sheet. Her face was half turned away. It looked haggard and emaciated. The nocturnal light spilling into the room through a narrow slit in the curtains seemed to have got caught in all the wrinkles. Egger fell asleep, and when he woke again the teacher was curled up on her side and he could hear her soft crying, muffled by the pillow. For a while he lay there beside her, irresolute, but then he realized there was nothing in this world that could be done about it. He got up quietly and left.

That same year a new teacher came to the village, a young man with a boyish face and shoulder-length hair tied back in a little ponytail, who spent his evenings knitting jerseys and carving roots into small, twisted crucifixes. The quiet and discipline of the old days never returned to the school, and Egger got used to the racket behind his bedroom wall. He only saw the teacher Anna Holler once more. She was walking across the village square with a shopping basket. She was walking slowly, with unnaturally small steps; her head was lowered, and she seemed to be completely lost in thought. When she saw Egger she raised her hand and waved to him with her fingers as you would to a little child. Egger quickly looked at the ground. Afterwards he was ashamed of this moment of cowardice.

Anna Holler left the village as quietly and inconspicuously as she had arrived. One cold morning, before sunrise, she climbed aboard the post bus with two suitcases, sat down in the back seat, closed her eyes, and, as the driver later reported, didn't open them again once throughout the journey.

That autumn the snow came early. Just a few weeks after Anna Holler's departure the skiers were already forming long queues outside the valley stations, and the metallic click of ski bindings and the creak of ski shoes could be heard all over the village until late into the evenings. One cold, clear, sunny day shortly before Christmas, as Egger was on his way home after taking a few elderly hikers for a walk in the snow, a group of excited tourists, followed by a few locals, the village policeman and a horde of screeching children, came walking towards him on the other side of the street. Two young men in ski suits had converted their skis into a kind of stretcher, and on it lay something that could evidently only be transported with the utmost care. The men were handling this something with a curious reverence that reminded Egger of the zeal of servers creeping round the altar during Sunday Mass. He crossed the street to take a closer look at the spectacle, and what he saw stopped his breath. On the makeshift stretcher lay Horned Hannes.

For a moment Egger thought he must have gone mad, but there was no doubt about it: before him lay the goatherd, or what was left of him. His body was frozen solid. From what Egger could see he appeared to be missing one leg, while the other stuck out over the side of the stretcher, grotesquely dislocated. His arms were wrapped tightly around his chest; dried scraps of flesh hung from his hands, and the bones of his fingers, almost entirely exposed, were crooked like the talons of a bird. His head was tilted right back on his neck, as if someone had yanked it violently backwards. The ice had torn half his face off the bone. His teeth in the blue-black gums were exposed and it looked as if he was grinning. Although both eyelids were missing, the eyes were completely intact and seemed to be staring, wide open, at the sky.

Egger turned away, took a few steps, stopped again. He felt sick and there was a dark buzzing in his ears. He wanted to say something to the men – but what? The thoughts danced in his head. He couldn't formulate any of them, and by the time he turned again they had long since moved on. They were right at the bottom of the street, proceeding towards the chapel with their icy burden. On one side walked the policeman. On the other the goat-herd's leg jutted up into the air like a withered root.

A couple of adventurous cross-country skiers had found Horned Hannes off-piste in a crevasse high in the Ferneis glacier. It took them hours to hack him out of the perpetual ice. The narrowness of the crevasse had, for the most part, kept birds and other animals away, and the ice had preserved his body through the decades. Only the leg was missing. The men speculated: perhaps an animal had got it before he slipped into the crevasse – perhaps a rock had cut it off – perhaps he had severed it himself in an act of desperation, to try and free himself. The mystery could not be solved: the leg had disappeared, and the stump revealed nothing. It was just a stump, coated in a delicate layer of ice, slightly frayed around the edges and blue-black in the centre like the goatherd's gums.

The dead man was brought to the chapel so that every-one who wanted to could say goodbye. But no one came, apart from a few tourists who wanted to see with their own eyes the mysterious ice-corpse laid out by candlelight, and if possible to photograph it from every angle. No one knew Horned Hannes, no one could remember him, and as the weather forecast predicted a rise in temperature he was buried the following day.

Egger was profoundly shocked by this unexpected encounter. Almost a whole life lay between Horned Hannes' disappearance and his turning up again. In his mind's eye he saw the translucent figure moving away in great leaps and disappearing into the white silence of the blizzard. How had he made it to the glacier several kilometres away? What had he been looking for there? And what had happened to him in the end? Egger shuddered at the thought of the leg that was probably still stuck somewhere in the glacier. Perhaps in a few years it too would be found and carried down to the valley as an outlandish trophy on the shoulders of excited skiers. Horned Hannes presumably didn't care about any of this. Now he lay in earth instead of ice: either way, he was at peace. Egger thought of the innumerable dead during his time in Russia. The grimaces of the corpses in the Russian ice were the most dreadful thing he had seen in his life. Horned Hannes, by contrast, seemed strangely happy. In his final hour he had laughed up at Heaven, thought Egger, and hurled his leg down the Devil's throat as a forfeit. This idea pleased him: there was something comforting about it.

But there was another thought that preoccupied him. The frozen goatherd had looked at him as if through a window in time. There was something almost youthful in the expression on his face, turned up towards Heaven. Back then, when Egger found him in his hut, mortally ill, and carried him down to the valley on the wooden frame, he must have been about forty or fifty years old. Egger was now well over seventy, and he certainly didn't feel any younger. Life and the work on the mountain had left their mark. Everything about him was warped and crooked. His back seemed to be heading down towards the earth in a tight curve, and he increasingly had the feeling that his spine was growing up over his head. On the mountain his foothold was still firm, and not even the strong autumn downwinds could make him lose his balance, but he stood like a tree that was already rotten inside.

* * *

In his final years Egger did not take up any more offers of work, which in any case became increasingly infrequent. He felt that in his life he had toiled enough; besides, he found the tourists' chatter and their moods, which changed as constantly as mountain weather, increasingly hard to tolerate. On one occasion he almost boxed the ears of a young townie, who stood on a rock and, overcome with joy, closed his eyes and turned round and round in circles until he plummeted onto the gravel field below and had to be carried back down to the valley by Egger and the rest of the group, sobbing like a little child. After that, Egger ended his career as a mountain guide and retired from public life.

The population of the village had tripled since the war, and the number of guest beds had increased tenfold, which prompted the municipality to proceed not only with the construction of a holiday resort with an indoor swimming pool and spa garden, but also with the long-overdue extension of the school building. Egger moved out before the construction workers even arrived. He packed his few possessions and moved into a cattle shed several hundred metres above the end of the village, abandoned decades earlier. The shed was worked into the hillside like a cave, with the advantage that the temperature wasn't subject to much fluctuation throughout the year. The front was constructed out of piled-up, weathered boulders. Egger filled the holes between them, first with moss, then with cement. He sealed the cracks in the door, painted the wood with pine tar, and scratched the rust off the hinges. Then he broke two stones out of the wall and replaced them with a window and a pipe for the sooty black stove he had found on a scrap heap behind the valley station of the Bubenkogel chair lift. He felt at ease in his new home. Sometimes it was a little lonely up there, but he didn't regard his loneliness as a deficiency. He had no one, but he had all he needed, and that was enough. The view from the window was good, the stove was warm, and once the shed had been heated throughout the first winter, if not before, the pungent smell of goats and cattle would have completely disappeared. Above all, Egger enjoyed the quiet. Only a faint suggestion reached him of the noise that now filled the whole valley and, at weekends, surged against the mountainsides in waves. Sometimes, on summer nights, when the clouds hung heavy over the peaks and the air smelled of rain, he would lie on his mattress and listen to the sounds of animals burrowing through the earth above his head; and on winter evenings he heard the muffled drone of the distant snow groomers preparing the pistes for the following day. He often found himself thinking about Marie. About what had been, and about what could have been. But they were just brief, fleeting thoughts that drifted by as quickly as the shreds of storm clouds outside his window.

As there was no one else for him to talk to, he talked to himself, or to the things around him. He'd say: 'You're useless. You're too blunt. I'm going to sharpen you on a stone. And then I'm going to go down to the valley and buy some fine sandpaper and sharpen you again. And I'm going to wind some leather around your handle. You'll sit nicely in the hand. And you'll look good, too, although that's not the point, you understand?'

Or he'd say: 'This weather makes you miserable. Nothing but fog. Your gaze slips because it doesn't know what to hang on to. If it carries on like this the fog'll soon come creeping into my room, and it'll start to drizzle ever so lightly over the table.'

And he'd say: 'Spring'll be here soon. The birds have seen it already. Something's stirring in the bones, and the bulbs are already splitting deep down beneath the snow.'

Sometimes Egger had to laugh at himself and his own thoughts. He would sit there alone at his table, look out of the window at the mountains with the shadows of clouds passing silently across them, and laugh until his eyes filled with tears.

Once a week he went down to the village to get matches and paint, or bread, onions and butter. He had realized long ago that people there speculated about him. When he set off for home with his purchases on his home-made sledge, which he upgraded with little rubber wheels in spring, he would see them out of the corner of his eye, putting their heads together and starting to whisper behind his back. Then he would turn around and give them the blackest look of which he was capable. Yet in truth he didn't much care about the villagers' opinions or their outrage. To them he was just an old man who lived in a dugout, talked to himself, and crouched in a freezing cold mountain stream to wash every morning. As far as he was concerned, though, he had done all right, and thus had every reason to be content. He would be able to live well for quite some time on the money from his tour-guiding days; he had a roof over his head, slept in his own bed, and when he sat on his little stool outside the front door he could let his gaze wander until his eyes closed and his chin sank onto his chest. In his life he too, like all people, had harboured ideas and dreams. Some he had fulfilled for himself; some had been granted to him. Many things had remained out of reach, or barely had he reached them than they were torn from his hands again. But he was still here. And in the mornings after the first snowmelt, when he walked across the dew-soaked meadow outside his hut and lay down on one of the flat rocks scattered there, the cool stone at his back and the first warm rays of sun on his face, he felt that many things had not gone so badly after all.

It was at this time, the time after the snowmelt, when in the early hours of the morning the earth steamed and the animals crept forth from their holes and caves, that Andreas Egger met the Cold Lady. He had tossed and turned on his mattress for hours, unable to sleep. Later he lay there quietly, arms folded over his chest, and listened to the sounds of the night: to the restless wind, prowling about the hut and knocking on the window with muffled thumps. Suddenly there was silence. Egger lit a candle and stared at the flickering shadows on the ceiling. He extinguished the candle again. For a while he lay there without moving. Finally he got up and went outside. The world was submerged in impenetrable fog. It was still night, but somewhere behind this soft silence day was dawning and the air shimmered like milk in the darkness. Egger took a few steps up the slope. He could hardly see the contours of his hand before his eyes, and when he stretched it out in front of him it looked as if he were plunging it into a deep, fathomless body of water. He walked on, carefully, step by step, a few hundred metres up the mountain. Far away he heard a note, like the long-drawn-out whistle of a marmot. He stopped and looked up. The moon hung in a gap in the fog, white and naked. Suddenly he felt a breath of air on his face, and the next moment the wind was back again. It came in solitary gusts, picking the fog to pieces, shredding it and chasing it apart. Egger heard the wind howling as it swept around the rocks higher up the mountain, and whispering in the grass at his feet. He walked on through streaks of fog that scattered before him like living creatures. He saw the sky open up. He saw flat rocks with remnants of snow on them, as if someone had covered them with white tablecloths. And then he saw the Cold Lady, crossing the slope about thirty metres above him. Her form was completely white, and at first he mistook her for a wisp of fog, but a moment later he clearly recognized her pale arms, the threadbare shawl that hung around her shoulders, and her shadow-like hair above the whiteness of her body. A shiver ran down his spine. Suddenly now he felt the cold. But it wasn't the air that was cold: the cold came from inside. It sat deep in his heart, and it was horror. The figure was heading for a narrow rock formation, and although it was moving swiftly Egger couldn't see it taking any steps. It was as if some hidden mechanism in the rock were drawing it on. He didn't dare move. The horror sat in his heart, yet at the same time he was strangely afraid that he might chase the figure away with a noise or a hasty movement. He saw the wind catch her hair, exposing, for a brief moment, the nape of her neck. And then he knew. 'Turn around,' he said. 'Please, turn around and look at me!' But the figure kept on receding, and Egger saw only the nape of her neck and the reddish sickle of her scar shimmering upon it. 'Where have you been so long?' he cried. 'There's so much to tell you. You wouldn't believe it, Marie! This whole, long life!' She didn't turn around. She didn't answer. All he heard was the noise of the wind, the howling and sighing as it swept across the ground, taking with it the last snow of the year.

Egger stood alone on the mountain. He stood there for

a long time without moving, as the shadows of the night slowly retreated around him. When he finally stirred, the sun was flashing from behind the distant mountain ranges and pouring its light over the mountaintops, so soft and beautiful that had he not been so tired and confused he could have laughed for sheer happiness.

Over the following weeks Egger roamed again and again across the rocky slopes above his hut, but the Cold Lady, or Marie, or whoever the apparition may have been, never showed herself to him again. Gradually her image faded until at last it dissolved entirely. Egger was in any case growing forgetful. Sometimes he would get up in the morning and spend over an hour looking for the shoes that he had hung on the stovepipe to dry the night before. Or, thinking about what he had wanted to cook for dinner, he would fall into a kind of brooding reverie so exhausting that he would often fall asleep sitting at the table, head propped on both hands, without having eaten a bite. Sometimes, before going to bed, he would place his stool next to the window, gaze out, and hope that against the backdrop of the night specific memories would surface that might bring at least a little order to his confused mind. More and more often, though, the sequence of events would slip away from him, things would tumble over one another, and as soon as an image seemed to come together in his mind's eye it would drift away again or evaporate like lubricating oil on hot iron.

Some people in the village thought old Egger was completely mad, certainly since a couple of skiers had seen him walk out of his hut stark naked one frosty winter morning and stamp about barefoot in the snow, trying to find a beer bottle he had left outside to cool the previous night. It didn't bother him. He was aware of his increasing confusion, but he wasn't mad. Besides, he barely cared what people thought any more, and as the bottle did in fact reappear after a brief search (right next to the gutter – it had burst overnight in the frost and he was able to suck the beer like a lolly on a stick), he considered with quiet satisfaction that, on this particular day at least, his reasoning and conduct had been justified.

According to his birth certificate, which in his opinion wasn't even worth the ink on the stamp, Egger lived to be seventy-nine years old. He had held out longer than he himself had ever thought possible, and on the whole he could be content. He had survived his childhood, a war and an avalanche. He had never felt himself to be above doing any kind of work, had blasted an incalculable number of holes in rock, and had probably felled enough trees to heat the stoves of an entire town for a whole winter. Over and over again he had hung his life on a thread between heaven and earth, and in his latter years as a tour guide he had learned more about people than he was able fully to understand. As far as he knew, he had not burdened himself with any appreciable guilt, and he had never succumbed to the temptations of the world: to boozing, whoring and gluttony. He had built a house, had slept in countless beds, stables, on the backs of trucks, and even a couple of nights in a Russian wooden crate. He had loved. And he had had an intimation of where love could lead. He had seen a couple of men walk about on the Moon. He had never felt compelled to believe in God, and he wasn't afraid of death. He couldn't remember where he had come from, and ultimately he didn't know where he would go. But he could look back without regret on the time in between, his life, with a full-throated laugh and utter amazement.

Andreas Egger died one night in February. Not somewhere out in the open, as he had often imagined he would, with the sun on the back of his neck or the starry sky above his brow, but at home in his hut, at the table. The candles had gone out and he was sitting in the faint light of the moon, which hung in the small square of the window like a light bulb dimmed by dust and spider's webs. He was thinking about the things he was planning to do over the next few days: buy a couple of candles, seal the draughty crack in the window frame, dig a ditch in front of the hut, knee-deep and at least thirty centimetres wide, to divert the meltwater. The weather would cooperate, he could say that with relative certainty. If his leg gave him some peace of an evening, the weather usually stayed calm the following day, too. He was overcome by a feeling of warmth at the thought of his leg, that piece of rotten wood that had carried him through the world for so long. At the same time he was no longer sure whether he was still thinking this, or was already dreaming. He heard a sound, very close to his ear: a gentle whisper, as if someone were speaking to a little child. 'I suppose it is late,' he heard himself say, and it was as if his own words hovered in the air in front of him for a few moments before bursting in the light of the little moon in the window. He felt a bright pain in his chest, and watched as his body sank slowly forwards and his head came to rest with his cheek on the tabletop. He heard his own heart. And he listened to the silence when it stopped beating. Patiently he waited for the next heartbeat. And when none came, he let go and died.

Three days later the postman found him when he knocked on the window to bring him the parish news-letter. Egger's body had been well preserved by the wintry temperatures, and it looked as if he had fallen asleep over breakfast. The funeral took place the following day. The ceremony was short. The parish priest froze in the cold as the gravediggers let the coffin down into the hole they had scraped out of the frozen ground with a little excavator.

Andreas Egger lies next to his wife, Marie. His grave is marked by a rough-hewn limestone veined with cracks, and the pale purple toadflax grows on it in summer.

Not quite six months before his death, Egger had woken up one morning with an inner restlessness that drove him out of bed and out of doors the moment he opened his eyes. It was the beginning of September, and where the sun's rays stabbed through the blanket of cloud he could see the gleam and flash of the commuters' cars: people who for some reason couldn't make a living in tourism and so threaded their way along the road every morning to arrive on time at their workplaces beyond the valley. Egger liked the look of this colourful string of cars snaking its way along the short stretch of road before its contours finally blurred and vanished in the misty light. At the same time, the sight of it made him sad. He thought of the fact that, apart from trips to the Bittermann & Sons cable cars and chair lifts in the surrounding area, he had only left the neighbourhood on one single occasion: to go to war. He thought about how once, along this very road, back then little more than a deeply rutted track across the fields, he had come to the valley for the first time on the box of a horse-drawn carriage. And at that moment he was overcome with a longing so searing and profound he thought his heart would melt. Without looking back he got up and ran. He limped, stumbled, raced down to the village as fast as he could, where the yellow number 5 bus – the so-called Seven Valley Line – was waiting at the stop outside the lofty Post Hotel with its engine running, ready to depart. 'Where to?' asked the driver, without looking up. Egger knew the man: he had worked for a few years fitting ski bindings in the repair shop run by the former

A Whole Life

blacksmith, until arthritis twisted his joints and he found work with the bus company. The steering wheel looked like a little toy tyre in his hands.

'To the last stop!' said Egger. 'You can't go further than that.' He bought a ticket and sat in an empty seat at the back amid the tired villagers – some of whom he knew by sight – who either didn't have the money for a car of their own, or were already too old to master its speed and technique. His heart beat like mad as the doors closed and the bus drove off. He sank back in his seat and closed his eyes. For a while he stayed like that, and when he sat up and opened his eyes again the village had vanished and he saw things passing by along the road. Little boarding houses that had sprung up out of nowhere in the fields. Service stations. Petrol signs. Advertising hoardings. A guesthouse with bedding hanging from every single one of its open windows. A woman standing at a fence with one hand on her hip, her face indistinct, blurred by cigarette smoke. Egger tried to think, but the torrent of images made him tired. Just before falling asleep he tried to recall the longing that had driven him from the valley, but there was nothing there. For a moment he thought he could still feel a slight burning round his heart, but he was imagining it, and when he woke again he could no longer remember what it was he wanted or why he was sitting on this bus at all.

At the last stop he got off. He took a few steps across an expanse of concrete overgrown with weeds, then stopped. He didn't know which direction to go in. The square where he was standing, the benches, the low station building, the houses behind it all meant nothing to him. He took another faltering step, and stopped again. He was shivering. In his hasty departure he had forgotten to put on a jacket. He hadn't thought to pick up a hat, and he hadn't locked the hut. He had simply run off, and he regretted that now. Somewhere far off he could hear the babble of voices, a child being called, then the slamming of a car door, an engine growing louder and then rapidly fading away. Egger was now shivering so hard he would have liked to have something to hang on to. He stared at the ground, not daring to move. In his mind's eye he saw himself standing there, an old man, useless and lost, in the middle of an empty square, and he was more ashamed than he had ever been in his life. Just then he felt a hand on his shoulder, and when he slowly turned around the bus driver was standing before him.

'Where exactly is it you want to go?' the man asked. Old Egger just stood there, desperately searching for the answer.

'I don't know,' he said, and slowly shook his head, over and over again. 'I simply don't know.'

On the return journey Egger sat in the same seat he had picked for his departure from the valley. The driver had helped him on to the bus and accompanied him all the way to the back without asking for the return fare, or indeed saying anything at all. Although Egger didn't fall asleep this time, the journey seemed shorter to him. He felt better now: his heartbeat slowed, and when the bus dipped into the blue shadow of the mountains for the first time, the shivering stopped as well. He looked out of the window, not really knowing what he should think or feel. It was so long since he'd been away that he'd forgotten what it felt like to come home.

When they reached the stop in the village, he nodded farewell to the driver. He wanted to get home as quickly as possible, but when he had left the last houses behind, and all that lay ahead was the stair-like ascent to his hut, he succumbed to a sudden impulse and turned left onto a steep, little-used path that wound around a nameless, moss-green pond before snaking all the way up to the Glöcknerspitze. For a while he followed the path along a row of wire fences the municipality had erected to protect the village from avalanches; then he stepped through a narrow crevice, secured by iron bars driven deep into the rock, and finally crossed the Karwiesen meadow in its shady hollow. The grass was damp and gleaming, and a smell of decay rose up from the earth. Egger moved fast: walking came naturally to him, he had forgotten his tiredness and barely felt the cold. He had the sense that with every step he left behind him something of the loneliness and despair that had gripped him down on that unfamiliar square. He heard the blood rushing in his ears and felt the cool wind, which dried the sweat on his forehead. He had reached the lowest point of the hollow when he saw a barely perceptible movement in the air. A little white something, dancing directly in front of his eyes. A second later, another. The next moment the air was filled with innumerable tiny scraps of cloud, floating slowly down and sinking to the ground. At first Egger thought they were blossoms the wind had blown in from somewhere, but it was September already and nothing blossomed any more at this time of year, certainly not this high up. And then he realized it was snowing. The snow fell thicker and thicker from the sky, settling on the rocks and the lush green meadows. Egger walked on. He paid close attention to his footsteps, taking care not to slip, and every few metres he wiped the snowflakes from his lashes and eyebrows with the back of his hand. As he did so a memory rose up in him, a fleeting recollection of something very long ago, little more than a blurred image. 'Not just yet,' he said, quietly; and winter settled over the valley.

picador.com

blog
videos
interviews
extracts